Library of
Davidson College

GLYPH 5

Editors: Samuel Weber and Henry Sussman
Editorial Board: Alicia Borinsky, Rodolphe Gasché, Carol Jacobs, Richard Macksey, Louis Marin, Jeffrey Mehlman, Walter Benn Michaels, Eduardo Saccone
Editorial Assistant: Marilyn Sides

GLYPH
JOHNS HOPKINS TEXTUAL STUDIES

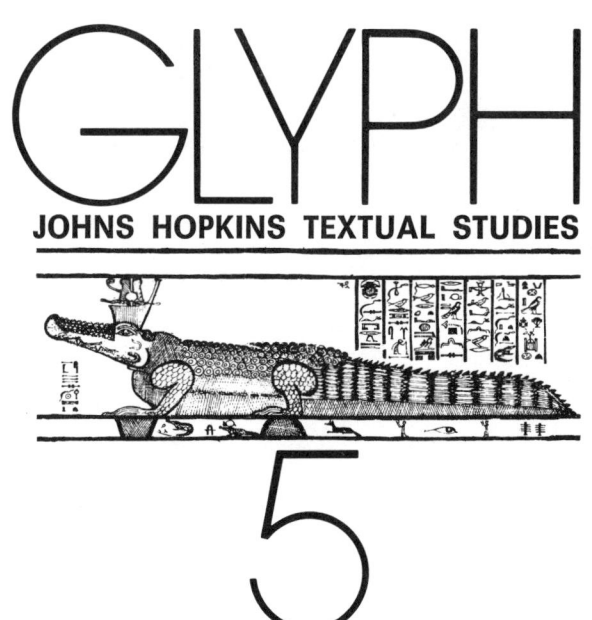

5

THE JOHNS HOPKINS UNIVERSITY PRESS
Baltimore and London

COPYRIGHT © 1979 BY THE JOHNS HOPKINS UNIVERSITY PRESS
All rights reserved. No part of this book may be reproduced or transmitted in any form or by any means, electronic or mechanical, including photocopying, recording, xerography, or any information storage and retrieval system, without permission in writing from the publisher. Manufactured in the United States of America
The Johns Hopkins University Press, Baltimore, Maryland 21218
The Johns Hopkins Press Ltd., London
Library of Congress Catalog Card Number 76-47370
ISBN 0-8018-2192-4 (hardcover)   ISBN 0-8018-2193-2 (paperback)

STATEMENT TO CONTRIBUTORS

The Editors of *Glyph* welcome submissions concerned with the problems of representation and textuality, and contributing to the confrontation between American and Continental critical scenes. Contributors should send *two* copies of their manuscripts, accompanied by return postage, to Samuel Weber, Editor, *Glyph*, Humanities Center, The Johns Hopkins University, Baltimore, Maryland 21218. In preparing manuscripts, please refer to *A Manual of Style*, published by the University of Chicago Press, and *The Random House Dictionary*. The entire text, including extended citations and notes, should be double-spaced.

Copies of *Glyph*, both hardbound and paperback, may be ordered from The Johns Hopkins University Press, Baltimore, Maryland 21218.

The illustration on the cover and title page, an Egyptian crocodile from the Ptolemaic period, is reproduced through the courtesy of the Walters Art Gallery, Baltimore.

CONTENTS

ONE   The Discourse of the Other: Hölderlin's Ode "Stimme des Volks" and the Dialectic of the Enlightenment
RAINER NÄGELE   1

TWO   *Grazia, Sprezzatura*, and *Affettazione* in Castiglione's *Book of the Courtier*   EDUARDO SACCONE   34

THREE   Plexed Artistry: Aratean Acrostics   WILLIAM LEVITAN   55

FOUR   A "Raft of Trouble": Word and Deed in *Huckleberry Finn*   LAURENCE B. HOLLAND   69

FIVE   Cotton Mather's Crazed Wife
MITCHELL ROBERT BREITWIESER   88

SIX   On Literature and Condensation: Robert Musil's Early Novellas   PETER HENNINGER   114

Notes on Contributors   133

GLYPH 5

ONE

THE DISCOURSE OF THE OTHER: HÖLDERLIN'S ODE "STIMME DES VOLKS" AND THE DIALECTIC OF THE ENLIGHTENMENT
Rainer Nägele

THE UNCERTAIN position that Hölderlin occupies in German literary history testifies to the uneasiness that his texts produce. There is today no dearth of admirers and interpreters, however. To the contrary, what made Hölderlin an outsider to his contemporaries appears to have made him the contemporary of modern readers, in poetic practice no less than in textual theory. It is precisely their apparent obliqueness with respect to the historical context which has given his texts the ability to stimulate a critical discourse in France for the same reasons that such a discourse arose from Mallarmé's texts, for example, and that has had its effect on modern poetic practice from the late Rilke to Paul Celan. The categories of hermeticism and poetic closure that are often applied in this context only describe such a quality inadequately—all the more inadequately in Hölderlin's case, since the intentionality of his texts, as opposed to that of his epoch, is aimed at the public sphere, just as it is committed to a concept of poetry better suited to the spectators at the sports arenas of Pindar than to the private study in which the subject believes that it is at home alone with the text and with itself.

No doubt it was precisely this addressing of the poetic text to a public context that was bound to close it off—to the extent that the public sphere for which it was designed did not exist—or, more exactly, to the extent that the public sphere was reduced to the act of consumption that devours the text. What Habermas has analyzed as structural change in the public sphere is not exterior to these texts, but is rather inscribed in their genesis. Even in its activity of "speaking-to" (*Ansprechen*), the "address" (*Anspruch*) of Hölderlin's text is deflected before the open jaws and closed eyes. In their attempt to speak to history directly, these texts encounter a yawning emptiness; wounded and astonished, they questioningly revert back to themselves. What results from the reflection upon history, to which and about which they want to speak, is a reflection of the text upon itself. And it is this moment of self-reflection which, despite all the differences, brings these texts into the proximity of some modern texts and which makes them so capable of being addressed by a critical discourse concerned with the problematic of textuality and contextuality.[1]

The interpreting text cannot exclude itself from this problematic; the question as to the place of the discourse and its subject concerns the interpretation to no lesser degree. Both the place that Habermas assigns the text within the public sphere and the displacement that the text undergoes in Lacan's psychoanalytic discourse occur as poetic processes in a text by Hölderlin, one which stimulated the reading suggested here and, at the same time, became readable insofar as the interpreting text sought its own place, led on by the mediating and displacing text of Freud.

A text that at the end of the decade following the French Revolution even hesitantly equates the voice of the people with the voice of God: such a text demands a hearing. But it is remarkable that almost no reference has been made to "Stimme des Volks"* in the intensive discussion surrounding Hölderlin's coming-to-terms with the French Revolution, though it would appear to belong at the center of such a discussion. To the contrary, in the few interpretations of this text its concrete historical and political implications are scarcely mentioned. Nonetheless, it takes part in a general discourse that touches upon the fundamental questions in the interpretation of the French Revolution, as it raises the issue of that problematic subject of the revolution, the people. But when the question is posed in this way it simultaneously implies the question of the interpreter's discourse, and it is this point that Hölderlin's text, after repeated revision, finally reaches:

---

* See Appendix 2 for two revisions of the poem.

3
Hölderlin's Ode "Stimme des Volks"

> And no doubt the sagas have worth, for they
> Are a memorial to the highest, but still
> It takes someone to interpret the holy sayings.[2]

A very similar textual process can be traced in yet another ode. Among the short, two-strophe odes that Hölderlin sent to Neuffer in the summer of 1798, we find the poem "To the Germans" (An die Deutschen); alongside "Voice of the People." The former poem thematizes the problematic behavior of the people (in this case, the Germans) who, since they are "rich in thoughts and poor in deeds," try the patience of the poet. The solution to the problem is left even more open here than it is in "Voice of the People." And so this poem too undergoes a reworking around 1800, one that ultimately goes so far that the poem "To the Germans" becomes the ode "Rousseau." In terms of textual process, this apparently radical thematic shift corresponds precisely to the shift in "Voice of the People": direct historical reflection arrives at the point at which it becomes aware of the problematic of its own discourse, and the text enters into a reflection about itself. But this should not be seen as a flight from history, but rather as an act of reflection upon that which is involved in the relation of the text to history. It leads in the late Hölderlin to a dialectic in which history appears as a text that inscribes itself in the mute wilderness of the world, while the poetic text becomes the hermeneutic act that attempts to decipher the writing of history. However, the problematic of this intertextuality consists in the fact that the hermeneutic-poetic discourse and the discourse of history do not occupy the same plane—or more precisely—that they, being internally ruptured, carry the unceasingly contradictory discourse of the one and the other within themselves. It would be tempting to formulate this contradiction in terms of the dichotomy of rationality/irrationality. But that would bring the reading back to the very field which Hölderlin's text forces open, in order to indicate another field of speaking in which, as false alternatives, the categories rational/irrational become otiose. Nevertheless, for the purposes of reading it is not unimportant to note the temptation. The fact that it exists indicates the still dynamic potency of the field from which the text sets itself apart, but to which it continues to relate in exactly the same measure as it is set apart. The text proceeds from a historically codified dichotomy in order to suspend it (*um sie aufzuheben*).

Even the first short version of the ode includes a complex constellation of relational tensions: the discourse of the one who says "I"[3] in this case still implies a resistance in the emphatic acceptance and recognition of the voice of the people as "God's voice." In the ". . . yes and I say it still" we find formulated an element of doubt that the equivalence (people/God) encounters in the articulated subject ("I"). The following verses indicate the problematic: namely, that the discourse of this "voice of the people" pursues a course that is different from the sequence of thought in which the "I" moves. A further tension is indicated between the current opinion-giving (*Meinen*) of the "I" which articulates itself in the "saying" and the earlier intonation of "sacred youth" which in its form as "premonition" already belongs to a different sphere, one that obviously does not exist in the articulate domain of rational discourse, but, precisely because it takes this form, possibly stands closer to the "voice of the people." Actually, in the semantic domain of the voice of the people and that of the earlier discourse of the "I," recognized only against its own apparent resistance, a sphere becomes defined that we might cautiously describe as *a-rational*.

In this connection, the plane of metaphor is of special interest, since it is here that the recognition and acceptance of the voice of the people through the comparison with a natural phenomenon is enacted. Thereby the voice becomes set apart (*abgesetzt*) from the rational discourse of a reasoning "I." Once again, this is in keeping with a long tradition and leads us at the same time directly into the political and poetic use of metaphor at the time of the French Revolution.[4]

The provenance of the saying "vox populi, vox dei," upon which Hölderlin bases his poem, has not been explained. Friedrich Beißner alludes to a similar concept in Hesiod (*StA* II, 495). But the suppression and repression of the plebeian voice was usually more pronounced than its divinization. Alcuin, in a letter to Charlemagne, offers a polemic against what, even in his time, were apparently well-known words concerning the voice of the people and the voice of God: "Nec audiendi, qui solent dicere: Vox populi, vox DEI. Cum tumultuositas vulgi semper insaniae proxima sit."[5] The people's mode of expression appears here as a nonarticulated "tumultuositas," whose placement within the domain of insanity pushes the *vox populi* out of the realm of rational discourse. The unpredictability of plebeian utterances has been a literary and rhetorical topos since antiquity. But with the

5
Hölderlin's Ode "Stimme des Volks"

French Revolution the topos acquires a new, intensive meaning in and through political events, and it is here that the use of metaphors drawn from nature plays a central role. There are countless examples in which the revolutionary masses appear in images of volcanic eruptions, fires burning out of control, floodwaters overflowing dikes, and wild animals. Thereby, however, the nature metaphor carries out a double function that is in keeping with the basic ambivalence in the concept of nature during the eighteenth century. Nature, that is, can serve both the sympathizers and the opponents of revolution. What for the opponents becomes the phantasmic display of an anxiety that sees in the behavior of the popular masses the madness of unrestrained natural forces is seen by the sympathizers as the expression of a purifying nature that completely washes or burns away the evils of society. Thunderstorms are especially popular, as in a poem by Klopstock on the French Revolution:

> As the sultry stillness [announces]
> The storm that whirls the thunderclouds before it
> Till they become a fire massed—become ice that blasts and wastes.
> After the storm they scarcely breathe, the winds, the brooks
> Murmur, little drops fall from the leaves,
> A freshness fills the air, the odors go round, the aetherial blue
> Smiles and the heavenly painting with her. . . .
>
> [Wie die schwüle Stille den Sturm
> Der vor sich her sie wirbelt, die Donnerwolken, bis Glut sie
> Werden und werden zerschmetterndes Eis.
> Nach dem Wetter atmen sie kaum, die Lüfte, die Bäche
> Rieseln, vom Laube träufelt es sacht,
> Frische labet, Gerüch' umduften, die bläuliche Heitre
> Lächelt, das Himmelsgemälde mit ihr. . . .][6]

Carl Philipp Conz celebrates the "Constitutional Festival in France"[7] with the river metaphor:

> That is where my ecstatic spirit today resides,
> Drawn on by high feelings as one with theirs engaged,
> There the call whose thunder the air divides,
> Like torrents rushing, like the cataract enraged. . . .
>
> [Da weilet heute mein entzückter Geist,
> Von hohem Mitgefühle angezogen,
> Vom Ruf, der donnernd dort die Luft zerreißt,
> Gleich der empörten Katarakte Wogen. . . .]

The despots have fallen away from nature itself, while the revolutionaries restore nature: "Rebels there, separated from nature" (*Rebellen dort, mit der Natur entzweit*), "Nature and Justice are ruling" (*Natur und Recht regiert*). Thereby the relationships become reversed to a certain extent: the despots are the rebels—indeed, they are rebels against nature, while the rebels represent both justice and nature. According to the Hölderlin of the Tübingen period, the discourse of the tyrants becomes an impotent chatter before the order of nature:

> Can the dictates of tyrants banish the oceans?
> Can the dictates of tyrants restrict the stars' course?
>
> [Kann Tyrannenspruch die Meere bannen?
> Hemmt Tyrannenspruch der Sterne Lauf?] (*FA* II, 166)

But the ease with which this use of metaphor can have its polarity reversed is demonstrated in an exemplary way by one of Lavater's poems, to which the disillusioned Swiss himself later wrote a parody. In the first version the French Revolution is greeted enthusiastically. The rulers appear as the metaphorical beasts of prey: "That no minister's tiger-tooth/Will devour the marrow of the land again?" (*Daß kein Minister-Tigerzahn/Mehr Mark des Landes frißt?*).[8] In the parody the persons are simply interchanged; now it is the "freedom-crier—tiger-tooth" (*Freiheitsrufer—Tigerzahn*). In Schiller's "Lied von der Glocke" it is the "dames" (*Weiber*) gone wild who become "hyenas" and tear apart the heart of their enemies "with panther's teeth" (*mit des Panthers Zähnen*). Not only the grotesque image, but also the surreal conflation of images (hyenas with panther-teeth!) signal a condition of extreme anxiety.

Thus the image becomes the rhetorical topos that is designed to engender anxiety once more. Already in 1789, Schubart sees the people tear apart their "torturers with tiger's rage" (*Peiniger mit Tigergrimm*).[9] For Huber the revolutionary "dames" (*Weiber*) who supposedly "knew no happiness other than lust" (*kein Glück als Wollust kannten*) become "furies."[10] The entire political situation appears to him to exist within the state of uproarious nature: "The thunder yet growls below you;/Your earthly kingdom is ruled by sea-wave" (*Noch brüllt der Donner unter dir;/Dein Erdreich wallt die Meereswogen*).[11] The use of weather metaphors enters entirely different dimensions in Blake. The pathos of apocalypse transcends mere rhetorical denunciation. The ruled and the rulers are overarched by and at the same

Hölderlin's Ode "Stimme des Volks"

time participate in a natural-historical process in which elemental nature and history appear as *one* power. The actors are historical subjects, but they are transcended by their actions. When the king, saddened by recent events, enters the "chamber of council" it is, at the same time, a natural event:

> Troubled, leaning on Necker, descends the King to his
> chamber of council; shady mountains
> In fear utter voices of thunder; the woods of France embosom
> the sound;
> Clouds of wisdom prophetic reply, and roll over the palace
> roof heavy.[12]

The historical figures in Blake do not speak, but are spoken instead. At the same time, however, just as in Hölderlin, the texts of Blake lay bare that which "plays along," in a nonconceptualized way, in the most shopworn rhetorical formulations of the day.

The use of nature metaphors is one expression of that deep-seated ambivalence which, in the eighteenth century, finds in nature the liberation from social and political constraints and in natural discourse the liberation from the bonds of what is felt to be the oppressive rule of reason, on the one hand, and, simultaneously, fears the unleashing of that which might free itself from repression and oppression.

The political implications become especially clear in those bourgeois intellectuals of Germany who moved from an initial enthusiasm for the revolution to a position of rejection. Significantly, the Jacobins, above all, were considered to be the hobgoblins of the Revolution; according to a contemporary writer, they placed "sovereignty in the will of the people" (*die Souveranität in den Volkswillen*).[13] The enthusiasm of many of the Revolution's sympathizers was based upon a conceptualization in which the subject of the Revolution was pictured as a gathering of reasoning, enlightened, and morally upright individuals. Any deviation of the real popular movement from this conception produced anxiety and postures of defense.

A quite abstract and idealized conception also dominates the young Hölderlin for a time. The early hymns of Tübingen portray the struggle for freedom as a process that is, indeed, fired by the enthusiasm of high ideals, but is also harmonious in the long run. Nevertheless, as Christoph Prignitz has shown in what is to date the best-documented work on Hölderlin's coming-to-terms with the French Revolution, the impression made by the real events going on in France introduced a new element to the scene: the positive reception of "chaos" as a necessary element in the over-all process.[14] To be sure, the threatening power of the chaotic—threatening in terms of one's own discourse—is held in check by the historical progression, which continues to be postulated in a well-organized and orderly fashion. But the disharmonious element has intruded itself, and it now leads to a concretization of the concept of *Zeitgeist*, which is itself elevated to the level of the "God of the times." The political implication of this emphatic recognition of the *Zeitgeist* as one of the highest beings becomes evident when one takes into consideration the role that this concept, precisely, plays in the conservative criticism of the revolution (and still plays in the conservative vocabulary). As a paradigm of this criticism, one can cite the verses of Gleim, who denounces the "spirit of the times" in the following words:

> He [the *Zeitgeist*] is the most hateful of all the spirits of this earth;
> He calls himself a patriot,
> And his friends are the bloodthirstiest
> Hangmen of all! A club's his murder weapon!
>
> [Er ist der häßlichste von allen Erdengeistern;
> Er nennt sich Patriot,
> Und seine Freunde sind von allen Henkermeistern
> Die Blutbegierigsten! Er schlägt mit Keulen tod!][15]

Moreover, Gleim does not hide his feelings about the voice of the people. In his poetic response to Klopstock's enthusiastic ode on the Etats Généraux he writes:

> So, you don't want any more than twelve hundred
> Despots, eh? Ha! I'm amazed that you who've taken
> such a shine to despotism don't want still more of their kind.
> . . . .
> If *one* got too mad for you,
> Him, I think, you could get under control:
> What's more, the wrath of *one* can't be inherited:
> Twelve hundred, though, are no longer mortal.
>
> The wise man, I think, that's my opinion,
> Gets along best in one man's dominion.

9
Hölderlin's Ode "Stimme des Volks"

[Nicht mehr als etwa nur zwölfhundert
Despoten wollt ihr? Ha! mich wundert
Daß ihr, der Despotie so hold!
Nicht mehr noch ihrer haben wollt?
. . . .
Den *Einen* macht' er's euch zu toll,
Den, dächt' ich, zwänge man noch wohl;
Auch ist des *Einen* Wuth nicht erblich:
Zwölf *hundert* aber sind nicht sterblich.

Der Weise, dächt' ich, sollt' ich meinen,
Der hielt es immer mit dem *Einen*!][16]

Here it is interesting to note not only how the revolutionary topos of the "wrath" (*Wut*) of the tyrant is transferred over onto the people but also how Gleim, almost paralleling Hölderlin's ode, opposes the discourse of the sage to the tumult of the people and, in the redundancy of "I think," "that's my opinion" emphatically asserts the prerogative of this discourse (in contrast to Hölderlin).

The peculiar thing in Hölderlin's coming-to-terms with the *Zeitgeist* and the voice of the people is not, however, that he simply puts the pure, positive recognition in place of the denunciation, but rather that he, in the hesitancy of his recognition, simultaneously reflects the tension and difference between his own discourse and that of the other. However, while in the earlier two-strophe version the problematic is only marked as difference, and, indeed, as a difference that not only shows itself between the "I" and the voice of the people, but also appears within the "I" itself, the later revision fully develops the reflection, as the text seeks to articulate this difference more precisely and to further ground it. Thereby, a remarkable uncertainty, or even contrariety, appears in the specification of this difference and in that which the "I" expects from the voice of the people. On one side a destructive desire for death (*Todesdrang*) appears which, in the third version, leads to a collective suicide; on the other, a self-satisfied tranquillity emerges that does not wish to commit itself through action. It is not too difficult to recognize herein the schematized problematic of two historical experiences: on the one hand, the French revolutionary movement (or whatever had been precipitated from it in public discourse) and, on the other, the failure of the German revolutionary movement to achieve fruition.

But one notices, at the same time, that these two historical modes of behavior, one French, one German, do not at all appear as separate alternatives in the textual process, but rather merge, comprehended as one movement, in the identical negativity of death. But now, with regard to this negativity, Hölderlin's text does not simply find itself taking the side of positive opposition, but demonstrates an attitude similar to that demanded by Hegel in the foreword to the *Phenomenology of Spirit*:

> It [the *Geist*] only wins to its truth when it finds itself in utter desolation. It is this mighty power, not by being a positive which turns away from the negative, as when we say of anything it is nothing or it is false, and, being then done with it, pass off to something else; on the contrary, mind [the *Geist*] is this power only by looking the negative in the face, and dwelling with it.

> [Er (der Geist) gewinnt seine Wahrheit nur, indem er in der absoluten Zerrissenheit sich selbst findet. Diese Macht ist er nicht als das Positive, welches von dem Negativen wegsieht, wie wenn wir von etwas sagen, dies ist nichts oder falsch, und nun, damit fertig, davon weg zu irgend etwas anderem übergehen; sondern er ist diese Macht nur, indem er dem Negativen ins Angesicht schaut, bei ihm verweilt.][17]

The three versions of the text of "Voice of the People" are marked by a steadily growing tendency to dwell with the negative. The difficulty of reading is closely connected with this tendency or, more precisely, with the dialectic of textual process, which can be circumscribed as stillness in movement and as movement that desires to be stilled. This difficulty of reading becomes paradigmatically evident in Wolfgang Kayser's interpretation. Kayser's reading is subtle enough, however, to gain a sense of the dialectic which constitutes the text and to articulate it as a structural dialectic: "Two modes of thought have revealed themselves: a thought in correspondences (conjunction: also), and a thought in oppositions (conjunction: nonetheless, but)."[18] Nevertheless, he forgets this dialectic due to the anecdotal proclivities of the text and attributes the loss of memory to the text itself: "Due to the portrayal of the one-time happening we almost forget its exemplarity, and the narrator has done the same. For the spiritualized formula he offers in strophe sixteen, 'It is not advisable to mock heroes,' does not fit logically in the context. We are concerned here neither with heroes nor defiance, but rather with participation, with the day of festival."[19] Thereby the text becomes fixed precisely at that point where it does not allow itself to be fixed: in one of its phases. Participation and the day of festival are not everything. If some of them had "one festive day" like no other, it is nonetheless "surer" and "greater" "to travel the overarching course" (*StA* II, 50, ll. 42–48). Resistance and defiance are just as much problems of the text as participation and self-sacrifice.

The difficulty of the reading is intensified by the difficulty experienced when one attempts to describe the reading process itself. A portrayal of this process that recapitulates each and every step in that process would be conceivable. Such a portrayal, however, is always fictive with respect to the actual process of reading, since it pretends that the process of reading begins with the process of writing, while, in reality, the reader at the moment of writing has moved through the text at least once and usually more often. The sequence of the interpreted text is never the simple sequence of the written text. This is not a marginal reflection in regard to a text where the emphasis has been centrally and precisely placed upon the overarching course and the displaced, decentered chain of all events, insofar as that chain is remembered and articulated as history.

The sequence of the text therefore becomes the first concrete difficulty faced in reading, and it cannot be cleared out of the way with the "law of tone-changes" formulated by Hölderlin. The difficulty cannot even be specified immediately. Apparently, it requires only a small effort to recognize a poeto-*logical* nexus whose basic principle turns out to be the comparison between the course of the rivers flowing into the sea and the human urge to return to the origin. This basic principle is only slightly complicated by the double movement of the text through correspondences and oppositions, as noted by Wolfgang Kayser. But that too can be understood and conceptualized without much difficulty. Yet, nonetheless, it is precisely here, on the plane of connecting conjunctions (from which Kayser reads the double principle) that the deceptions of the text begin. When one takes a closer look, it becomes evident that the conjunctions themselves appear to waver in their function. This becomes especially clear in the conjunction which, by its insertion at the beginning of the third strophe, constitutes the text by continuing the two original strophes: "for" (*denn*) (l. 9). At first reading, its function seems clear: logically speaking, to ground the movement of thought; poetologically, to establish the comparison to the course of the rivers:

> For in self-forgetfulness, too ready to fulfill
>   The god's wish, what's mortal too quickly seizes
>   And once, with an open eye upon
>   Its own path traveling
>
> The shortest course back into the cosmos,
>   So the river plunges downward. . . . (StA II, 49, ll. 9–14)

But it is precisely this connection which reveals itself to be most problematic. The relationship between the human trajectory and the course of the rivers is mediated by a "what" (*was*—later by an "it" [*es*]) (StA II, 51, l. 12) that is marked by two qualifying determinations: it is "mortal" (*sterblich*) and travels "its own path with an open eye" (*offnen/Auges auf eigenem Pfad*). The second of these determinations, toward which everything tends, would scarcely appear to be applicable to the comparison with the river. After all, an individualized (*eigenem* = own) consciousness (*offnen Auges* = with an open eye) is implied here. And it is precisely this which does not allow itself to be inferred about the rivers in Hölderlin's precise and consistent use of metaphor. Moreover, in the Rhein song, on the same metaphorical level of visuality, one reads: "but the blindest . . ." (*die Blindesten aber/* . . .) are "sons of the gods" (*Gottersöhne* . . .) (StA II, 143, ll. 40f). The correspondence between that which "travels the path with an open eye" and the river which, against its will, plummets from crag to crag without rudder is thus not as simple as it may at first appear. Clearly, the correspondence is only made possible inasmuch as that which travels with open eyes negates precisely this quality and in "self-forgetfulness" (*selbstvergessen*) follows "the uncanny yearning toward the abyss" (*wunderbaren Sehnen dem Abgrund zu*) (l. 17)—which is to say that it no longer travels, but rather plunges (*stürzt*). The correspondence is also an opposition. The same dialectic is articulated by the text in the relationship between men and gods. The longing for the abyss is nothing other than the "wish of the gods" (*Wunsch/Der Götter*), articulated through mankind. To fulfill this wish means the self-annihilation of humanity; but since it is only in human beings that the wish of the gods can be articulated, they (the gods) must, to a certain degree, reject the pious recognition of humanity in order to preserve themselves and deny their selves, even as they recognize the self of humanity and restrict human self-forgetfulness.

13
Hölderlin's Ode "Stimme des Volks"

The relationship between the discourse of the "I" and the voice of the people is anticipated, paradigmatically, in this model, as it is finally formulated in the first revision of the ode:

Because it is pious, I now honor the voice of the people,
   The quiet one, for the sake of the heavenly ones!
     Yet for the sake of gods and humanity,
        Let the voice not sleep—too gladly—forever. (*StA* II, 50, ll. 49–52)

In spite of the preparation provided by the model, the pointed paradoxicalness in which the relationship is here articulated is surprising. It is not so much the combination of distancing and recognition that the "I" observes with respect to the voice of the people which seems paradoxical, but rather the almost identical basis for both positions of the "I." The discourse of the people is projected onto the same field in which the gods appear, and thus the respectful position of the "I" takes the form of a rendering of homage. But, at the same time, the "I" acquires critical distance through the admonition: "Let the voice not sleep—too gladly—forever." And this too is brought forward in the names of the gods, indeed—and this is the decisive difference—the critical admonition is articulated "for the sake of the gods" *and* for the sake of "humanity." For the sake of the relationship (just now indicated in the model) between gods and human beings—a relationship that, as already mentioned, guarantees the identity and existence of both inasmuch as the constitutive ground for both lies, eccentrically, outside their "selves"—the direction of the immediate wish must turn itself around in terms of the opposition already described. The textual rhythmic stress upon the phrase "for the sake of" (in the German the *"willen"* is idiomatically weakened into a preposition) also directs the reader's attention to its derivation from a nominal form (but not without also identifying the substantive element as preposition, as relationship) and thereby to the difference between the two "groundings": *"Zu lieb"* and *"um . . . willen"* in the German. This difference marks a shift at the level of the wish's articulation, one that can be described in the traditional code as a shift from the emotive plane to that of reason.

The quality ascribed to the voice of the people, the "quiet" one, in this final strophe also seems surprising. Even though such a quality could be understood in the context of the times as the articulation of a discontent with the German situation ("rich in thought and poor in deed" [StA II, 9, l. 4]), it nonetheless seems remarkable as the final result of a specific text, whose theme may indeed be the search for tranquillity, but which, precisely, localizes this search in images of plummeting, tearing, hurrying, and breaking, that is, in a series of progressively intensified, even destructive, activities. As the explication of the historical context, the text attempts to sum up the eccentricity of the phenomena in *one* principle.

But it is obvious that the resolution found in the first revised draft of the poem is not satisfying. The final strophe of the second revision ends up in a different place:

That was the way the children heard it,
   And no doubt the sagas have worth, for they
     Are a memorial to the highest, but still
       It takes someone to interpret the holy sayings. (StA II, 53, ll. 69–72)

To be sure, the mixture of recognition and distantiation remains. But the subject of the distantiation is no longer a knowing "I," but rather an unspoken instance which speaks in the name of that which "it" needs. At the same time, the "voice" of the people has produced "sagas" which, on the one hand, make the speaking subject anonymous, and which, on the other hand, transcend the speaker's still implicit presence within the voice of the people and point to a discourse that, in temporal terms as well, comes from somewhere else.

The text appears to have arrived at this "somewhere else" through a merely anecdotal extension which illustrates "the uncanny yearning toward the abyss" and the "desire for death." But the anecdote accomplishes much more by introducing a new principle, a principle of repetition that marks not only the discourse, but also the historical activity as being "long . . . prepared for" and anticipated. Thereby the subject is also decentered in his activity, as the text now explicitly states: "And they were beside themselves" (StA II, 53, l. 57). The problematic of the subject, already emerging in the earlier versions, is now radicalized and leads to changes in details that are almost imperceptible. Where, in the first revision, those who early came to rest and were early sacrificed nonetheless have "gained *their* portion" (StA II, 50, l. 40), in the second revision they have only "found *a* portion" (StA II, 52, l. 40).

At this point it is possible to summarize the basic themes from what is, at first glance, a confusing alternation of themes and motifs:

Hölderlin's Ode "Stimme des Volks"

the desire for death, the problematic of the subject, and the principle of repetition, whose relation to memory has yet to be considered. As regards this thematic constellation, another text, written much later, would seem to demand attention in an almost importunate way: Freud's *Beyond the Pleasure Principle* (1920).[20] Of central significance, in this text, are the principles of a repetition compulsion and of a death-drive, both of which have far-reaching consequences for the problematic of the subject. That is why it was not accidental that Jacques Lacan made this essay the focus of his seminar on the "I" in Freud (1954/55).[21]

However, such parallels are, methodologically, not without a problematic of their own. One runs the danger of forcing a text into the categories of another discourse on the basis of a few superficial similarities. In this way, "forerunners" of whichever "modernism" one prefers can be mass-produced, and the less attention paid to history the better. Or, in an even more banal version, a limited, timeless universe of clichés about "man in general" is the result. But, on the other hand, it is precisely here that the reflection made earlier on the reading of the text allows itself to be widened, namely, that there is no reading that is not mediated by one that has already preceded it, no understanding that does not take place within the problematic playing out of translation from one text into another. The origin of reading, the first text, eludes the reader as much as the origin of language, which was sought so fervently in the eighteenth century. Perhaps the attentive reader has not failed to observe that the hesitancy with which we take note of the insistent parallel between these texts has led to that reflection at which Hölderlin's text itself arrived, that is, the need for and problem of explicating the sagas.

If the parallelism between the two texts were restricted to the general principles of a death-drive (*Todeslust* = desire for death in Hölderlin) and that of a repetition compulsion, this would be obvious enough, but would still remain somewhat abstract. A more precise reading, however, shows not only individual points of thematic similarities, but also a surprising parallelism in the process and in the strategy of both texts, something which is all the more remarkable inasmuch as they are not only divided from each other by a considerable historical distance, but are also separated by virtue of their discrete genres. We also are not dealing with a relationship between texts, where one text consciously refers to another, as is the case in Sophocles' *Oedipus* and Freud's concept of the Oedipus complex. Despite Freud's wide reading in the universe of literature, Hölderlin seems to have made little or no impression upon him. At stake, therefore, is not the proving of a most unlikely "influence." Another possibility would be to go back to Freud's own observation when he said that the poets had always known what he took pains to discover. But such a statement is only permissible at the end, not at the beginning, of the analytical process. If it is put at the beginning, then the result appears as that kind of pseudo-Freudian reading which translates literary texts into psychoanalytical categories without actually going through the analysis which constitutes these categories in the first place. Moreover, one would then be engaged in an activity that Freud warned against in regard to the interpretation of dreams when he pointed out that it was not the latent dream-thoughts, but rather the dream-work that was essential. Therefore, what is at stake here is not a Freudian reading of Hölderlin's text, in whatever way such a reading is ordinarily understood, but rather a reading that puts both texts into contact with each other—indeed, one that begins by asking about the strategy and process of the texts.

It seems advisable to proceed from the question of difference between genres, a question that is all too often overlooked when poetic texts are translated into the categories of a theory. Even at this level a curious homology between both texts becomes evident in their difference. Both take their respective textual genre to the limit of its possibilities and do so with the help of certain means specific to each genre. Hölderlin uses the means at his disposal in the ode— above all, narrative inserts and reflective discourse—to such an extent that the dominance of the lyric element, which molds and shapes the genre, begins to falter. In no lesser way, Freud's text, with the help of the game-rules of the discursive-scientific text, underplays that which constitutes such a text. On the one hand, the text is based on a terminology that derives from the natural sciences; on the other, it is precisely these sections of the text that stand in the shadow of Freud's own warning: "What follows is speculation, often far-fetched speculation, which the reader will consider or dismiss according to his individual predilection. It is further an attempt to follow out an idea consistently, out of curiosity to see where it will lead."[22] To be sure, this warning about speculation more likely constitutes a diversion, itself a common rhetorical strategy *within* traditional scientific discourse, a discourse that is being placed in question on a completely different, more radical level: on the level of the speaking subject.[23] It is on this plane that both texts come into contact with each other.

In each case, narrative passages within the text play a central role. Their position within the respective texts is, however, different and points to the historical differences existing between them. While in Hölderlin the narrative segment only appears toward the end of the text's development, Freud's text opens up after a short, general introduction by way of a few case histories—more precisely, a few mentions of cases and a narration. It thus appears that Hölderlin's narrative is of a purely illustrative nature, and this would seem to fit both the poetic genre of the text and the historical context, which is to a large extent determined by speculative and deductive thought. On the other hand, Freud's text, in the tradition of the natural-scientific thought that gained ascendancy in the nineteenth century, puts the empirical case at the beginning and thereby assigns the narrative an evidentiary function that is scientific in nature. Nonetheless, as already noted in the Hölderlin text, the narrative can hardly be said to exhaust itself in its illustrative function. Rather, it introduces what is essentially a new principle that actually makes it possible to articulate the question that is inherent in the text. Conversely, Freud's anecdote about a child's game which, aside from the cases of accident- and war-neurosis only mentioned in passing, by itself constitutes the actual narrative, is much too singular and isolated to have the quality of an inductive proof. Rather, as in Hölderlin, it appears that it is precisely the particular case that effects the traumatic shock which creates the wound in the subject and places its discourse in doubt. Indeed, the narrative is only the anecdotal articulation of the shock and uncertainty that reveals itself at the beginning of both texts. Both begin in a surprisingly analogous way with a backward glance at opinions which, up till now, have been taken for granted. Hölderlin's text has been quoted already. Freud's essay begins: "In the theory of psycho-analysis we have no hesitation in assuming that the course taken by mental events is automatically regulated by the pleasure principle. We believe, that is to say, that the course of those events is invariably set in motion by an unpleasurable tension. . . ."[24] The pleasure principle, which is accepted in the theory without hesitation, is not done away with in the hesitant text, but it is forced to occupy a different position due to the new principles which have been hesitantly introduced. But, as new as these principles are, on the one hand, what remains just as valid for Freud's text as for Hölderlin's is that the thing which is hesitantly recognized does not represent something absolutely new, but rather something which has already revealed itself in anticipation. Hölderlin's text is, on the explicit level, a coming-to-terms with that which he anticipated and believed "in sacred youth." In Freud's text, which in a certain sense grounds the later, meta-psychological writings, striking similarities between it and some of the earliest preanalytic writings of Freud have been found.[25] The principle of memory that thematizes both texts also appears to be a principle in their genesis.

The process of these two texts is, then, (re)marked by the grounding (*Begründung*) of a destabilizing and decentralizing tendency in discourse, one whose onsets are discontinuous. Between the texts, points of thematic contact can be found in certain details that go beyond the general principles already articulated. In Hölderlin, the play of active and passive voices appears as a moment of the process that initiates the repetition:

> . . . Their fathers too, when they
> Were once *seized* in the past and sorely pressed
>   By the Persian foe,
>
> Set fire to the reeds in the river—*seizing* them
> So that they might break free in the open city.
>   (emphasis mine, StA II, 53, ll. 62–66)

This transformation of the passive into the active, which in Hölderlin first articulates itself at the end of the text's development, in Freud becomes an initial phase in the interpretation of the child's repetitive game: "On an unprejudiced view one gets an impression that the child turned his experience into a game from another motive. At the outset he was in a *passive* situation—he was overpowered by the experience; but, by repeating it, unpleasurable though it was, as a game, he took an *active* part."[26] To be sure, there is an essential difference between both actions. Hölderlin's historical paradigm, which obviously serves him as a paradigm for his own time, points to an act of liberation that finally winds up in an aporia. Those who here make themselves into acting subjects by changing from the "seized" into the "seizing" in order to "break free" seize nothing but that which destroys them, as concrete subjects. This formulation seems pregnant with the findings which Lacan, in his essay "Le stade du miroir," included in his critique of existential philosophy:

> At the end of the historic venture on the part of a society to grant itself no function that is not useful, and in the face of the individual's anxiety before social contacts within the masses, whose rise seems to be the reward of that venture, existentialism can be judged by the justifications it gives to the subjective dead-ends that result therefrom: a freedom that affirms itself nowhere as authentically as within the walls of a prison, a demand for engagement in which the inability of the pure consciousness to surmount a given situation expresses itself, a voyeuristic–sadistic idealization of the sexual relationship, a personality that realizes itself only in suicide, a consciousness of the other that can only rest content once it has committed the Hegelian murder.[27]

It is not accidental that Hölderlin has also been made into the mouthpiece for all sorts of existentialisms. Indeed, this is only possible where and when the text is treated apart from its hesitant ambivalence and "fixed." To the extent, in this case, that the action of the poem is acknowledged as an articulation of the people, it is simultaneously problematized as articulated "saga."

At the end of the text a further category is introduced that has a bearing on this problematic: repetition not as pure activity, but as discourse (*Sagen*) and remembrance (*Gedächtnis*). Now this is the case with which Freud concerns himself in his discussion of the child's game, one which already represents repetition as symbolic gesture and as discourse (o-o—a-a). What has been accomplished here in a natural way is that which Freud wanted to achieve in psychoanalysis: to *remember* (*erinnern*) instead of *repeat* (*wiederholen*).[28] Formulated in Hölderlin's discourse, this means that in the end the wish of the gods appears in the form of the articulated sagas and of memory, which, indeed, signify no end, since the sagas again require explication. With all of this said, however, one should not attempt to dissimulate some sort of identity between the texts. It is their distance from each other that makes it possible for their reflective thought to converge at a single point outside themselves, in that focus which marks and problematizes the text as interpretation. At this point, Freud's text even joins Hölderlin's in the poetic register. Although the text with which Freud's discourse ends lies outside Freud's own discourse, it nonetheless articulates his problematic:

> What one cannot fly over, one must limp over.
> . . . .
> The scripture says it is no sin to limp.[29]

This is the point at which the third text—limpingly—comes in, the commentary, which, in the external focus already mentioned, meets up with the two others and attempts once more—in concluding before an ending that never takes place—to reflect back upon the text from which it proceeded, in order to arrive at that point from which it is speaking, or perhaps more precisely: will have spoken.[30] This, namely, is the question that Hölderlin's text puts to us in its historical context.

By problematizing the voice of the people, without asserting that it is false or that it is nothing, Hölderlin indeed places the course and discourse of history in question, but, even more than this, he places his own discourse in question, which, in the discrepancy between it and the discourse of the other, loses the authoritarian self-certainty of its own wisdom. But this should by no means be taken to mean, as the secondary literature sometimes maintains, that Hölderlin stands against the Enlightenment. To the contrary, what cannot be emphasized too strongly is the extent to which his "train of thought," precisely, is (pre)marked by the discourse of the Enlightenment. It is not accidental in his texts that, in those very instances in which the discourse turns to moments of utopian fulfillment, key words of the Enlightenment frequently crop up. One need only think of the final verse of the fifth strophe of "Stutgard":

And a people with premonitions rises upward all-mighty—
  Till the youths remember their fathers on high
    The enlightened human being stands before you illumined,
                       a child no more.

[Und allmächtig empor ziehet ein ahnendes Volk,
  Bis die Jünglinge sich der Väter droben erinnern,
    Mündig und hell vor euch steht der besonnene Mensch.] (StA, II, 86)

Nevertheless, that Enlightenment is criticized which postulates its adulthood, brightness, and illumination in a self-certain manner, before it has recognized the conditions of its own discourse. The problematic of the reasoning bourgeois, who declares himself to be a rational subject and human being, has been documented exhaustively by Habermas in his study on structural changes in the public sphere, where he shows how pretensions regarding a universal public were undermined by a practice that excluded a large portion of the public sphere, the "voice of the people," from discourse. Moreover, where rational discourse sets an absolute line of demarcation in the codified dichotomy between rationality and irrationality, it displaces its own participation in both fields, one of which is subjected to the interdict of negation. A writer as early as Lenz caricatured such behavior in the figure of the Privy Councillor in his play, the *Hofmeister*. The discourse of the Privy Councillor, which in itself is quite reasonable, becomes absurd when confronted with the discourse of Läuffer, who is neither ready nor able to hear or understand it. Hölderlin broadens this critique so as to include the problematic of the poetic text, insofar as this is an articulation of history that goes beyond everything private. The recognition of the "voice of the people" in this context is the paradigmatic gesture of a text which, since it is conscious of its own inexpugnable contingency and transience, confirms itself by having continual recourse to the discourse of the other, and thus strives to attain what can only then be a truly rational discourse, one which would at the same time be the fulfillment of that which is poetic:

> Starting out from morning, man has experienced much—
> Since we are a conversation and can hear of each other—
> Soon, though, we'll be song.
>
> [Viel hat von Morgen an,
> Seit ein Gespräch wir sind und hören voneinander
> Erfahren der Mensch; bald sind wir aber Gesang.]
> ("Friendensfeier," *StA*, II, 356)

Translated by Robert G. Eisenhauer

APPENDIX 1

The immanence of this problematic with regard to the texts becomes discernible in the polemics that have been spun out around their periphery. While the historical and political dimension had been repressed for a long time, the belief came into circulation during the sixties that a Jacobin witness for one's own problematic *engagement* had suddenly been found in Hölderlin, the partisan of the Revolution. But, even as the texts were being studied at this time (but also missed to a certain extent), something began to emerge that was to have important consequences. If a new critical-historical edition of Hölderlin has been in preparation and publication for the past two years (moreover, in a left-wing publishing house), this is more than a mere academic event, yet it does not represent, as myopic academic criticism immediately maintained, a politicized falsification. The politicizing of the edition does not consist in its subordination of the texts to political opinions, but rather in its insistence upon literally showing, in the presentation of these texts, that process whereby both text and context are made problematic. Thereby the texts themselves are changed minimally, but the process of reading is greatly altered. The advantage the new Frankfurt edition, published at the Verlag Roter Stern, has over the Stuttgart edition resides in the literal laying-bare of a textual problematic that is hidden in the previous edition because of a prior editorial decision. Though both editions attempt to give an account of the text's genesis, the conception of this genesis varies in each case from the standpoint of approach. The Stuttgart edition, throughout, offers the "final" reading-text, printed by itself in attractive, large lettering, in a separate volume. The "variant readings" and "drafts" of the "final text," throughout, are printed separately in a volume containing the apparatus: they appear in smaller type-faces and are ordered chronologically according to a complex system of coded abbreviations. This technical mode of presentation implies nothing less than the ontologizing of the "final" and "closed" text, the one which declares all phases of its genesis to be teleologically suspended (*aufgehobenen*) "drafts" (should there be any later reworkings of a "final" text, as is the case with "Brod und Wein," these are treated as "late" and therefore already rather de-ranged (*verrückte*) deviations, deserving of no textual authority). The "reading text" that has been authorized in this fashion, to a certain extent, forces the reader (assuming that he even cares at this point about the genesis of the text) to read this genesis from that imaginary, but authoritarian end-point (which only in the rarest of cases represents a phase of the text that actually became apparent to Hölderlin himself).

By contrast, the Frankfurt edition begins with a photographic reproduction of the manuscripts (when extant) and then reproduces the spatial characteristics of the MS. in a diplomatic copy of the original. It then proceeds to an analysis of the phases in the text's development by converting the spatial pattern into a temporal sequence through the uses of various typefaces (whereby the unavoidable interpretative instance of the editor, as translator, is made explicit before the reader's eyes). From this point, the Frankfurt edition goes on to the constituted phases of the text—to "reading texts" in the sense of the Stuttgart edition—only in those instances where Hölderlin produced such a "finished" text himself. Thus the ontological phantasm of "the" text, whose beginning and end are clearly delimited, disappears from the reader's field of vision, and the reader instead finds himself faced with a process of signification that, while it may indeed be stabilized as a relatively autonomous entity at determinate intervals by means of a beginning and ending, also sets off this entity, as

23
Hölderlin's Ode "Stimme des Volks"

        Wo, wo leuchten sie deñ, die fernhintreffenden Sprüche(,)?

        Delphi schlumert und wo tönet das große Geschik?

        Wo ist das schnelle? wo brichts, allgegenwärtigen Glüks
                                      voll

20   Doñernd aus heite(t)rer Luft über die Völker herein?
                    riefs   **og**

        Vater Aether! so rufts und fliegt von Zunge zu Zunge,
                          ug

        Tausendfach, es erträgt keiner das Leben allein,

25   **geerbet von Eltern**

        Ausgetheilet erfreut solch Gut und gegeben, genomen
                                getauscht, mit Fremden
                                schlafend

        Wirds ein Jubel, es wächst (alternd) des Wortes Gewalt

30   **heiter!**   **weit es gehet, das uralt**

        Vater! Aether und hallt, so tief, so ewig die Nacht ist,
        Zeichen, von Eltern geerbt treffend
        So vermessen die Noth, (siegend) und schaffend hinab.
                                (den)

35   **tiefschütternd gelangt so aus Schatten**

        Deñ so kehren die Himlischen ein, so steiget (in) Nächten
        (Abgerungen) Aus den Schatten/
        Vorbereitet/herab unter die Menschen ihr Tag.
                          5.

        Unempfunden komen sie erst, es streben entgegen

40   Ihnen die Kinder, zu hell komet, zu blendend das Glük,

        Und es scheut sie der Mensch, kaum weiß zu sagen ein
                                        Halbgott,

From the Frankfurt edition, manuscript and transcription showing part of Hölderlin's early version and revision of a poem, *Brod und Wein*, later *Der Weingott*. Photo courtesy of Verlag Roter Stern.

literal *découpage*, from a context whose margins have once more been cut out. Reading all of this rids the reader of the beautiful, seeming order of "intrinsic" and "extrinsic" once and for all, and the simply stated admonition to the student to "read nothing but what is on the page" draws him into the swirl of a process of signification that allows no margins to endure and that irresistibly implicates the reader and his position with respect to the text.

APPENDIX 2

Hölderlin: "Voice of the People"
(first revision)

That you were God's voice: I believed it once,
   In my sacred youth—yes and I say it still!
      Heedless of our wisdom though
         The rivers too thunder on and yet,

Who does not love them? and my heart
   Is always touched by them—hearing the dwindling
      Ones, the ones full of premonition, take a different
         Course and hurry more surely into the sea afar.

For in self-forgetfulness, too ready to fulfill
   The god's wish, what's mortal too quickly seizes
      And once, with an open eye upon
         Its own path traveling

The shortest course back into the cosmos,
   So the river plunges downward seeking rest,
      But it grabs, it pulls him against his will
         From ledge to ledge—rudderless the river,

Drawn down by an uncanny yearning toward the abyss.
   And scarcely has it climbed up from earth when,
      On the same day, the cloud turns once again
         To its birth-place—weeping down from purpled height.

And the desire for death seizes peoples too,
   And the cities of heroes sink down; the earth greens
      And there before the stars, like people
         In prayer flung into the dust before

Those inimitable ones, lies the long art, over-
   Thrown in free-will; he himself, the human being,
      Dashed his own work and so gave
         Homage to the lofty ones.

25
Hölderlin's Ode "Stimme des Volks"

But they do not love mankind less for this;
   They love again, in equal measure, as they are loved,
     And often they restrict the course of man
        So that he might linger to rejoice in the light.

And like the eagle's brood, he himself,
   The father throws them from the nest, so that
     They will seek their prey in the field;
        The gods drive us out in a like way, with a smile.

Happy are they, they who have gone to rest,
   Who fell before their time; they too, they too
     Were sacrificed like the earliest harvest—
        They have gained their portion!

You did not go under, dear ones, without all
   The ecstasies of life. One festive day
     Was given you beforehand and the others
        Never found such a day.

Yet it is surer and greater and more than these
   Worthy of the mother, who is all to all,
     To travel the overarching course—hesitating in the
        Midst of hurry, borrowing the eagle's desire.

Because it is pious, I now honor the voice of the people,
   The quiet one, for the sake of the heavenly ones!
     Yet for the sake of gods and humanity,
        Let the voice not sleep—too gladly—forever.

Hölderlin: "Voice of the People"
(second revision)

That you were God's voice: I believed it once,
   In my sacred youth—yes and I say it still!
     Heedless of our wisdom though
        The rivers too thunder on and yet,

Who does not love them? and my heart
   Is always touched by them—hearing the dwindling
     Ones, the ones full of premonition, take a different
        Course and hurry more surely into the sea afar.

For in self-forgetfulness, too ready to fulfill
   The god's wish, what's mortal too quickly seizes,
     When with an open eye it once travels
        Upon its own paths,

Rainer Nägele

The shortest course back into the cosmos; so
  The river plunges downward seeking rest,
    But it grabs, it pulls him against his will
      From ledge to ledge—rudderless the river,

Drawn down by an uncanny yearning toward the abyss.
  What is unbound provokes and the people too
    Are seized by desire for death, while defiant
      Cities, after striving toward the best,

Driving on the work, year in, year out, are
  Struck down by a sacred finish; the earth greens
    And there before the stars, like people in
      Prayer, flung into the dust before those

Inimitable ones, lies the long art, overthrown
  In free-will; he himself, the human being,
    Dashed his own work and so gave
      Homage to the lofty ones.

But they do not love mankind less for this;
  They love again, in equal measure, as they are loved,
    And often they restrict the course of man
      So that he might linger to rejoice in the light.

And not only the eagle's brood are thrown from the nest
  By the father so that they'll not stay
    With him too long; we too are driven out
      With a timely thorn by the lord.

Happy are they, they who have gone to their rest,
  Who fell before their time: they too, they too
    Were sacrificed like the earliest harvest—
      They have found a portion.

In Greek times the city lay on the Xanthos,
  But now, as with the greater ones who rest there,
    It has moved through a fate
      From the holy light of day.

But they died—not in open battle—
  By their own hand. From the East to us
    Has come the uncanny tale of what happened
      There and horrifying it was.

The generosity of Brutus provoked them.
  For when the fire had broken out, he offered
    To help them, though he himself, as general,
      Laid siege before the gates.

27
Hölderlin's Ode "Stimme des Volks"

Yet the servants threw those he had sent
 From the walls. And then the fire grew livelier;
  They rejoiced and Brutus stretched
   Out his hands to them

And they were beside themselves. There was
 Shouting and jubilation. It was then that man and woman
  Threw themselves into the flames, while some children
   Leapt from rooftops, others to their fathers' blades.

Defiance of heroes is inadvisable. But it had long
 Been prepared for. Their fathers too, when they
  Were once seized in the past and sorely pressed
   By the Persian foe,

Set fire to the reeds in the river—seizing them
 So that they might break free in the open city.
  And the flame took both house and temple—dwellers too—
   Soared up with them to sacred aether.

That was the way the children heard it,
 And no doubt the sagas have worth, for they
  Are a memorial to the highest, but still
   It takes someone to interpret the holy sayings.

Stimme des Volks
Erste Fassung

Du seiest Gottes Stimme, so glaubt ich sonst,
 In heilger Jugend; ja und ich sag es noch!
  Um unsre Weisheit unbekümmert
   Rauschen die Ströme doch auch, und dennoch,

Wer liebt sie nicht? und immer bewegen sie
 Das Herz mir, hör ich ferne die Schwindenden,
  Die Ahnungsvollen, meine Bahn nicht,
   Aber gewisser ins Meer hin eilen.

Denn selbstvergessen, allzubereit, den Wunsch
 Der Götter zu erfüllen, ergreift zu gern,
  Was sterblich ist und einmal offnen
   Auges auf eigenem Pfade wandelt,

Ins All zurück die kürzeste Bahn, so stürzt
 Der Strom hinab, er suchet die Ruh, es reißt,
  Es ziehet wider Willen ihn von
   Klippe zu Klippe, den Steuerlosen,

Das wunderbare Sehnen dem Abgrund zu,
 Und kaum der Erd entstiegen, desselben Tags

Kehrt weinend zum Geburtort schon aus
    Purpurner Höhe die Wolke wieder.

Und Völker auch ergreifet die Todeslust,
    Und Heldenstädte sinken; die Erde grünt
        Und stille vor den Sternen liegt, den
            Betenden gleich, in den Staub geworfen,

Freiwillig überwunden die lange Kunst
    Vor jenen Unnachahmbaren da; er selbst,
        Der Mensch, mit eigner Hand zerbrach, die
            Hohen zu ehren, sein Werk, der Künstler.

Doch minder nicht sind jene den Menschen hold,
    Sie lieben wieder, so, wie geliebt sie sind,
        Und hemmen öfters, daß er lang im
            Lichte sich freue, die Bahn des Menschen.

Und wie des Adlers Jungen, er wirft sie selbst,
    Der Vater, aus dem Neste, damit sie sich
        Im Felde Beute suchen, so auch
            Treiben uns lächelnd hinaus die Götter.

Wohl allen, die zur Ruhe gegangen sind
    Und vor der Zeit gefallen, auch sie, auch sie
        Geopfert gleich den Erstlingen der
            Ernte, sie haben ihr Teil gewonnen!

Nicht, o ihr Teuern, ohne die Wonnen all
    Des Lebens gingt ihr unter, ein Festtag ward
        Noch Einer euch zuvor, und dem gleich
            Haben die anderen keins gefunden.

Doch sichrer ists und größer und ihrer mehr,
    Die allen alles ist, der Mutter wert,
        In Eile zögernd, mit des Adlers
            Lust die geschwungnere Bahn zu wandeln.

Drum weil sie fromm ist, ehr ich den Himmlischen
    Zu lieb des Volkes Stimme, die ruhige,
        Doch um der Götter und der Menschen
            Willen, sie ruhe zu gern nicht immer!

Stimme des Volks
Zweite Fassung

Du seiest Gottes Stimme, so glaubt ich sonst
    In heilger Jugend; ja, und ich sag es noch!
        Um unsre Weisheit unbekümmert
            Rauschen die Ströme doch auch, und dennoch,

29
Hölderlin's Ode "Stimme des Volks"

Wer liebt sie nicht? und immer bewegen sie
    Das Herz mir, hör ich ferne die Schwindenden,
        Die Ahnungsvollen meine Bahn nicht,
            Aber gewisser ins Meer hin eilen.

Denn selbstvergessen, allzubereit, den Wunsch
    Der Götter zu erfüllen, ergreift zu gern,
        Was sterblich ist, wenn offnen Augs auf
            Eigenen Pfaden es einmal wandelt,

Ins All zurück die kürzeste Bahn; so stürzt
    Der Strom hinab, er suchet die Ruh, es reißt,
        Es ziehet wider Willen ihn, von
            Klippe zu Klippe, den Steuerlosen,

Das wunderbare Sehnen dem Abgrund zu;
    Das Ungebundne reizet und Völker auch
        Ergreift die Todeslust und kühne
            Städte, nachdem sie versucht das Beste,

Von Jahr zu Jahr forttreibend das Werk, sie hat
    Ein heilig Ende troffen; die Erde grünt
        Und stille vor den Sternen liegt, den
            Betenden gleich, in den Sand geworfen,

Freiwillig überwunden die lange Kunst
    Vor jenen Unnachahmbaren da; er selbst,
        Der Mensch, mit eigner Hand zerbrach, die
            Hohen zu ehren, sein Werk, der Künstler.

Doch minder nicht sind jene den Menschen hold,
    Sie lieben wieder, so wie geliebt sie sind,
        Und hemmen öfters, daß er lang im
            Lichte sich freue, die Bahn des Menschen.

Und, nicht des Adlers Jungen allein, sie wirft
    Der Vater aus dem Neste, damit sie nicht
        Zu lang ihm bleiben, uns auch treibt mit
            Richtigem Stachel hinaus der Herrscher.

Wohl jenen, die zur Ruhe gegangen sind,
    Und vor der Zeit gefallen, auch die, auch die
        Geopfert, gleich den Erstlingen der
            Ernte, sie haben ein Teil gefunden.

Am Xanthos lag, in griechischer Zeit, die Stadt,
    Jetzt aber, gleich den größeren, die dort ruhn,
        Ist durch ein Schicksal sie dem heilgen
            Lichte des Tages hinweggekommen.

Sie kamen aber nicht in der offnen Schlacht,
　Durch eigne Hand um. Fürchterlich ist davon,
　　Was dort geschehn, die wunderbare
　　　Sage von Osten zu uns gelanget.

Es reizte sie die Güte von Brutus. Denn
　Als Feuer ausgegangen, so bot er sich
　　Zu helfen ihnen, ob er gleich, als Feldherr,
　　　Stand in Belagerung vor den Toren.

Doch von den Mauern warfen die Diener sie,
　Die er gesandt. Lebendiger ward darauf
　　Das Feuer und sie freuten sich und ihnen
　　　Strecket' entgegen die Hände Brutus

Und alle waren außer sich selbst. Geschrei
　Entstand und Jauchzen. Drauf in die Flamme warf
　　Sich Mann und Weib, von Knaben stürzt' auch
　　　Der von dem Dach, in der Väter Schwert der.

Nicht rätlich ist es, Helden zu trotzen. Längst
　Wars aber vorbereitet. Die Väter auch,
　　Da sie ergriffen waren, einst, und
　　　Heftig die persischen Feinde drängten,

Entzündeten, ergreifend des Stromes Rohr,
　Daß sie das Freie fänden, die Stadt. Und Haus
　　Und Tempel nahm, zum heilgen Aether
　　　Fliegend, und Menschen hinweg die Flamme.

So hatten es die Kinder gehört, und wohl
　Sind gut die Sagen, denn ein Gedächtnis sind
　　Dem Höchsten sie, doch auch bedarf es
　　　Eines, die heiligen auszulegen.

NOTES

1. See Appendix 1.

2. Hölderlin's texts, where quoted, are from the following two editions of his works: Friedrich Hölderlin, *Sämtliche Werke*, ed. Friedrich Beißner (Stuttgart: Kohlhammer, 1943) and Hölderlin, *Sämtlich Werke: Frankfurter Ausgabe*, ed. Wolfram Groddeck (Frankfort: Roter Stern, 1975). Quotations from the Stuttgart edition (the larger Stuttgart edition) will be identified by the abbreviation *StA* and those from the Frankfort edition by *FA*. All translations of the poems in the text and the translations of "Stimme des Volks" in Appendix 2 are by Robert G. Eisenhauer.

3. The somewhat awkward formulation merely offers an expedient *solution*.

Hölderlin's Ode "Stimme des Volks"

At first I simply wanted to write "discourse of the subject," but now the equation of the "I" articulated in the text with the subject of the text seems all too problematic. The two are not equivalent. That which articulates itself as "I" is only a part of the subject, if not even the eccentric place, in which the subject is not at all. It might be possible to insert the traditional and (value-) neutral descriptive term "lyrical I," if this term were not, despite its apparent neutrality, weighted down with quite a lot of unarticulated ideological ballast that simply cuts off reflection upon the nature of that which is actually doing the speaking in the text. Below I speak either of the "articulated I" or, in abbreviation, of the "I", in order to remain aware of the "I's" partiality or eccentricity with respect to the subject of the text. It is hardly unimportant to note in the text discussed that the discourse of the articulated "I" departs, precisely, from the experience of its eccentricity.

    4. See Hans-Wolf Jäger, *Politische Metaphorik im Jakobinismus und Vormärz* (Stuttgart: J. B. Metzler, 1971) for a study that is rich in materials having to do with political metaphor.

    5. Quoted from Beißner's commentary on the ode: *StA* II, 495.

    6. *Deutsche Literatur in Entwicklungsreihen.* "Reihe Politische Dichtung," "Vor dem Untergang des alten Reichs:" *1756–1795*, I, 129. The poems in this volume offer an insight into almost all of the common political metaphors of the period.

    7. *Ibid.*, p. 143–46.

    8. *Ibid.*, p. 152.

    9. *Ibid.*, p. 113.

    10. *Ibid.*, p. 137.

    11. *Ibid.*, p. 139.

    12. William Blake, *Selected Poetry and Prose*, ed. Northrop Frye (New York: Modern Library, 1953), p. 106.

    13. *Neue Leipziger gelehrte Anzeigen für das Jahr 1794*: November 1, 1794.

    14. Christoph Prignitz, *Friedrich Hölderlin: die Entwicklung seines politischen Denkens unter dem Einfluß der Französichen Revolution* (Hamburg: Buske, 1976).

    15. Quoted by Prignitz, p. 246.

    16. Johann Wilhelm Ludwig Gleim, "Auch Les Etats généraux. An Frankreichs Demokraten," in *Epochen der deutschen Lyrik 1770–1800* (Munich: Deutscher Taschenbuch Verlag, 1970), p. 215 ff.

    17. Georg Wilhelm Friedrich Hegel, *Werke in 20 Bänden, Phänomenologie des Geistes* (Frankfort: Suhrkamp, 1970), 3, 36. English translation from *Hegel: Selections*, ed. Jacob Loewenberg (New York: Scribners, 1958), pp. 28–29.

    18. "Zwei Denkweisen haben sich enthüllt: ein Denken in Entsprechungen (Konjunktion: auch), und ein Denken in Gegensätzen (Konjunktion: dennoch, aber)." In *Die Deutsche Lyrik*, ed. Benno v. Wiese (Düsseldorf: A. Bagel, 1956), p. 386.

    19. "Uber der Darstellung des einmaligen Geschehens vergessen wir fast seine Beispielhaftigkeit, und auch der Erzähler hat es getan. Denn die Durchgeistigung, die er in Strophe 16 bringt: 'Nicht räthlich ist es, Helden zu trozen,' paßt nicht schlüssig in die Zusammenhänge. Es geht weder um Helden noch um Trotzen, sondern um die Teilhabe, um den Festtag." Ibid., p. 391 ff.

    20. All English versions of Freud's texts are taken from *The Standard Edition*

of the Complete Psychological Works of Sigmund Freud, translated by James Strachey in collaboration with Anna Freud (London: Hogarth Press, 1955), vol. 18. Quotations in German, as listed in the footnotes, are taken from S. Freud, "Jenseits des Lustprinzips," in Freud, *Studienausgabe,* Psychologie des Unbewussten (Frankfort: Fischer, 1975), 3: 213–72. The *Standard Edition* is abbreviated as *SE* throughout, the *Studienausgabe* text as *JL*.

21. Jacques Lacan, *Le séminaire.* Livre II: *Le moi dans la théorie et dans la technique de la psychanalyse* (Paris: Seuil, 1978).

22. *SE,* 24. "Was nun folgt, ist Spekulation, oft weitausholende Spekulation, die ein jeder nach seiner besonderen Einstellung würdigen oder vernachlässigen wird. Im weiteren ein Versuch zur konsequenten Ausbeutung einer Idee, aus Neugierde, wohin sie führen wird. (*JL,* p. 234)

23. On this point see J. Lacan's seminar (n. 20), as well as his essay "Die Wissenschaft und die Wahrheit," in Jacques Lacan, *Schriften II,* selected and edited by Norbert Haas (Olten/Freiburg: Walter, 1975), 231–57.

24. *SE,* p. 7. "In der psychoanalytischen Theorie nehmen wir unbedenklich an, daß der Ablauf der seelischen Vorgänge automatisch durch das Lustprinzip reguliert wird, das heißt, wir glauben, daß er jedesmal durch eine unlustvolle Spannung angeregt wird. . . ." (*JL,* p. 217)

25. See the editor's preliminary comments in the *Studienausgabe* of "Jenseits des Lustprinzips," p. 216.

26. *SE,* p. 16. " . . . bei unbefangener Betrachtung gewinnt man den Eindruck, daß das Kind das Erlebnis aus einem anderen Motiv zum Spiel gemacht hat. Es war dabei passiv, wurde vom Erlebnis betroffen und bringt sich nun in eine aktive Rolle, indem es dasselbe, trotzdem es unlustvoll war, als Spiel wiederholt." (*JL,* p. 226)

27. "Au bout de l'entreprise historique d'une société pour ne plus se reconnaître d'autre fonction qu'utilitaire, et dans l'angoisse de l'individu devant la forme concentrationnaire du lien social dont le surgissement semble récompenser cet effort, — l'existentialisme se juge aux justifications qu'il donne des impasses subjectives qui en résultent en effet : une liberté qui ne s'affirme jamais si authentique que dans les murs d'une prison, une exigence d'engagement où s'exprime l'impuissance de la pure conscience à surmonter aucune situation, une idéalisation voyeuriste-sadique du rapport sexuel, une personnalité qui ne se réalise que dans le suicide, une conscience de l'autre qui ne se satisfait que par le meurtre hégélien." Jacques Lacan, "Le Stade du miroir" in *Ecrits* (Paris: Editions de Seuil, 1966), p. 99.

28. "The patient cannot remember the whole of what is repressed in him, and what he cannot remember may be precisely the essential part of it. Thus he acquires no sense of conviction of the correctness of the construction that has been communicated to him. He is obliged to *repeat* the repressed material as a contemporary experience instead of, as the physician would prefer to see, *remembering* it as something belonging to the past" (*SE,* 18). "Der Kranke kann von dem in ihm Verdrängten nicht alles erinnern, vielleicht gerade das Wesentliche nicht, und erwirbt so keine Überzeugung von der Richtigkeit der ihm mitgeteilten Konstruktion. Er

ist vielmehr genötigt, das Verdrängte als gegenwärtiges Erlebnis zu *wiederholen*, anstatt es, wie der Arzt es lieber sähe, als ein Stuck der Vergangenheit zu *erinnern*" (*JL*, p. 228).

29. *SE*, p. 64. Was man nicht erfliegen kann, muß man erhinken.

(. . .)

Die Schrift sagt, es ist keine Sünde zu hinken. (*JL*, p. 272)

30. On the second future as a positioning of the subject see Samuel M. Weber, *Rückkehr zu Freud. Jacques Lacans Ent-stellung der Psychanalyse* (Frankfort, Berlin, Vienna: Ullstein, 1978), esp. p. 10 ff.

TWO

GRAZIA, SPREZZATURA, AND *AFFETTAZIONE* IN CASTIGLIONE'S *BOOK OF THE COURTIER*
Eduardo Saccone

Grazia, sprezzatura, affettazione: these three words have long claimed the particular attention of students of Baldesar Castiglione's *Courtier*. I set them out here again in an order to which we need not ascribe any special significance, though it may by the end acquire one. It should at any rate be apparent to any reader of this work that among these three there exists a connection—an interrelation and interdependence—even though it has generally been the first term of the trinity to be privileged as the object of investigation. Such examination may even have been excessive, and not without some unfortunate results, if we consider for example that many illustrious scholars have concentrated their attentions, not on the function of these terms in their proper context, but on the determination of the "concept" or "idea"— Castiglione's theory of grace, let's say—in the historic and philosophical setting of the Renaissance, or rather, by a more limited approach, in the context of so-called classical art theory. Thus it befell one preeminent student of the Renaissance, Eugenio Garin, in the fourth chapter of his well-known book *L'Umanesimo italiano*, entitled "Platonism and Philosophy of Love," in the second section dedicated precisely to the problem of grace, to refer to whom he calls "two great theorists of grace, Castiglione and Della Casa," and to involve himself in an attempt to make the "concept" of grace that our author holds, as the very cornerstone and premise of the *Book of the*

Courtier, depend on a Ficinian or more generally Neoplatonic matrix, by the use of arguments and especially of supportive texts that I cannot but consider dubious.¹ Again, much more recently, in an article appearing in the second volume of the *Dictionary of the History of Ideas*, Rudolph Wittkower first reviewed the *venustas* of classical authors from Cicero to Quintilian and the Elder Pliny, which he would have correspond to the more modern *grazia*, "the irrational element in works of art," that defies "rational analysis." Then he wrote: "From the XVI century onward classical art theory was permeated with this concept. 'Grace' for the Italians from Baldassare Castiglione to Vasari and beyond was *un non so che*, which in the French theory of the XVII century became the *je ne sais quoi* and in England, in Pope's immortal phrase: 'a grace beyond the reach of art'."²

Here again there is much that we might wish to question, but this is neither the time nor the place to do so. At present I am only concerned to indicate the perspective that interested this scholar, which is evidently that of the history of ideas: with respect to which the most significant study on our subject is without doubt the article by Samuel Holt Monk, to whose title and content Wittkower himself makes explicit reference. This article, drawing its title from just that phrase of Pope's cited above, appeared appropriately in the April 1944 issue of the *Journal of the History of Ideas*.³ Finally, I will mention, if only for the reputation of this often printed work, *Artistic Theory in Italy, 1450–1600* of Sir Anthony Blunt. In it we learn that Vasari, "the first writer to elaborate the theory of grace in connection with painting, . . . only applied to the arts the conception of grace as a necessary part of behaviour which had been evolved by the writers of manners, particularly those of the Neoplatonic school, such as Castiglione." Then, further on he writes: " 'Grace' is that extra quality which is added to the more solid 'properties' and 'conditions' which can be acquired by precept. Grace, on the other hand cannot be learnt; it is a gift from heaven; and it comes from having a good judgement." This Blunt attempts to clarify as follows: "It will vanish if a man takes too much pains to attain it, or if he shows any effort in his actions. Nothing but complete ease can produce it. And the only effort which should be expended in attaining it is an effort to conceal the skill on which it is based; and it is from *sprezzatura* . . . that grace springs."⁴

So grace is an "extra quality," that is not to be acquired by precept, since it is a gift from heaven. On the other hand, and here the logic of the argument escapes me, it derives from good judgement, from that effort to conceal skill that is *sprezzatura*. Again, I will not linger over the details, but only stop to point out the tendency of this argument, which like that of the others we have glanced at, is quite different from my present intention. It will be my endeavor not to limit the discussion to a relatively narrow semantic field, that of aesthetics, nor to reduce or abstract from the complex reality of the text, but to adhere to it as far as possible, grounding myself, as I have already suggested, not so much on the ideas, especially where these ideas have been rendered prematurely clear and distinct, but on the materials from which literary texts are made, and so on the words themselves. Beginning with these, then, and first of all, as we must, with *grazia*, even before considering its use in the *Courtier* it seems not inopportune to note the characteristic ambivalence of the word in Italian, and before that of the Latin *gratia*, from which it derives.

The broadest, most fruitful and complex definition, but also the most precise that I know—applicable as well to the Italian as the Latin—is to be found in the *Thesaurus Linguae Latinae*: "*gratia* proprie favorem significat, i. inclinationem animi ad bene faciendum alicui, colendum aliquid tam ultro quam ob beneficium ante acceptum. Hinc transfertur ad statum eius personae, cui hic favor accidit. Similiter de qualitate rerum, quae placent, adhibetur."[5] In insisting on the meaning of *gratia* as *favor*, this definition (as to some extent do all other dictionaries, both Latin and Italian) puts the stress on the semantic alternation, equally present in the Latin *gratus* and the Italian *grato*, made evident by the active and passive uses of the word. Thus, for example, an expression like "Io ti son grato" can mean either "I am welcome, or appreciated, I am acceptable to you," or "I feel gratitude towards you." The definition also points out the twofold value, abstract and concrete, of the term. *Grazia* is an attribute, or rather a gift, that presupposes two parties: one who attributes, gives, or offers, and another who takes, receives, or accepts; he who favors, and he who is favored. It is a process, an operation, therefore, that necessarily implies a beginning and an end, or rather, an intention and an object. It is interesting to note that this structure is substantially retained even in the specifically Christian usage of the word. The only real distinction is relatively unimportant in this context, though essential in its own: that is, that the two parties in Christian usage are specified as God and man, with the concomitant gratuitousness of the gift. What counts however is the retention of the structure. We may also remark that in either case there is a tendency to reify the term in a substance or a quality, in some more convenient and simplified identity that obscures its progressive character, so that the dynamism of a form disposed to accept any content according to the circumstances hardens until it conforms to a static and determinate content.

This semantic alternation is moreover explicitly recalled in the text, when Cesare Gonzaga declares "la forza del vocabulo" ("the very meaning of the word") by which "si po dir che chi ha grazia quello è grato" ("it can be said that he who has grace finds grace") as Professor Singleton translates.[6] On the other hand, in confirmation of the definition given in the *Thesaurus*, that insists, as we have seen, on the fundamental sense of *favor*, here is the first occurrence of the word in Castiglione's text, where it appears in significant relation to the final end immanent in the formation of the perfect courtier: "Now, you have asked me to write my opinion as to what form of Courtiership most befits a gentleman living at the courts of princes, by which he can have both the knowledge and the ability to serve them in every reasonable thing, thereby winning favor from them and praise from others [*acquistandone da essi grazia e dagli altri laude*]: in short, what manner of man he must be who deserves the name of perfect Courtier, without defect of any kind" (I, 1, Maier, pp. 79–80; Singleton, p. 11).

The grace that is here at issue is that of the prince and is to be distinguished from "praise," which ought to come from "others." In chapter vii of Book II this distinction appears to be reaffirmed: "noble birth," "talent," "bodily disposition, and comely aspect [*grazia dell'aspetto*]" are all very well, says Federico Fregoso, but more is required "to win praise deservedly, and a good opinion on the part of all, and favor from the prince whom he serves [*e grazia da quei signori ai quali serve*]" (Maier, p. 198, Singleton, p. 97). It appears, in other words, that we should here reserve for grace a specifically vertical relationship, one, that is, that moves exclusively in an up and down direction, from the prince to his courtier. This insistence should not be viewed as a casual component in the strategy of the book; certainly it anticipates the end of the courtier's profession as it is delineated in the fourth book, where the theory is set out of the courtier's function as counselor and almost preceptor to the prince, a situation that is obviously owing to the "favor acquired by his good accomplishments [*la grazia acquistata con le sue bone qualità*]" (IV, v, Maier, p. 451; Singleton, p. 289), as we read there. Thus grace becomes, from an end in itself, the means in turn to another and higher end, to that "good end [*bon fine*]," that is the education and direction of the perfect prince. Many other places in the text besides treat of the "grazia . . . dei principi," "grazia e favore" of the prince (as for example in IV, x, p. 458, and IV, vi, p. 452).

But that this distinction is strategic, and so serves a certain economy of the text without any general validity beyond it, can be demonstrated in another instance: "But in the end all these qualities in our courtier will still not suffice to win him universal favor with lords and cavaliers and ladies [*per acquistar quella universal grazia de' signori, cavalieri e donne*]" (II, xvii, Maier, p. 215; Singleton, p. 109). Now it is evident that the vertically limited lord–courtier direction we remarked before no longer pertains; a horizontal dimension has been added. The favor or grace desired here must come as well from "cavalieri e donne," that is to say, from the other members of the class to which the courtier belongs.

Up to this point, it will be noted, the examples I have listed have this in common: they all refer to the object, or rather the end, to the final moment of a process, the moment when grace is achieved (*acquistata*, the verb recurs in all these passages). We ought now to consider the other pole of the process, from the end to the beginning, as it were, or from the other to the self. But first we must clear up a difficulty owing to a neglected yet necessary distinction, that is at the heart of some noteworthy misunderstandings, and is certainly responsible for some ambiguities particularly evident in the critical passages cited above, especially those of Wittkower and Blunt. It will be recalled that the former spoke of grace in works of art as an "irrational element," a "*non so che*," while the latter went so far as to call it a "gift from heaven." Now the first step, and one that is essential to the pedagogical scheme of the *Courtier*, is to delimit an area, that can serve as an Aristotelian middle ground between two exceptional conditions, the "mean" between absolute perfection and imperfection, between "eccellente grazia" and "insensata sciocchezza" (I, xiv, p. 105).[7] One could perhaps even say that for Castiglione it was the middle territory between the divine and the brutish, and hence the territory that a humanist might consider specifically human. Within this scheme, that is, then, the only one in which we may speak of human sociability,[8] Don Ippolito d'Este, Cardinal of Ferrara, is called upon to play the part of the divine, or rather, of the representative of those who "seem not to have been born, but to have been fashioned by the hands of some god, and adorned with every excellence of mind and body" (I, xiv, Maier, p. 104; Singleton, p. 29). At the opposite extreme we find the "many others so inept and uncouth that we cannot but think that nature brought them into the world out of spite and mockery" (ibid.). Just as for the representatives of the first category the "summit of the highest excellence" is an attribute, an original grace, for the others, on the contrary, "assidua diligenzia e bona crianza poco frutto per lo più delle volte possono fare," the others "yield little fruit even with constant diligence and good care."

As I have already suggested, however, the discussion in the *Courtier* applies not to the especially gifted or the absolutely ungifted, but indeed to those who, without being "so perfectly endowed by nature," can nevertheless, "with care and effort, polish and in great part correct their natural defects" (ibid.). What is required, in other words, is a minimal but necessary basis from which to build, that will comprise, according to the *desideratum* of Ludovico da Canossa, "besides his noble birth, . . . [his being] endowed by nature not only with talent [*ingegno*] and with beauty [*bella forma*] of countenance and person, but with that certain grace which we call an "air" [*una certa grazia e, come si dice, un sangue*], which shall make him at first sight pleasing and lovable [*grato ed amabile*] to all who see him; and let this be an adornment informing and attending all his actions, giving the promise outwardly that such a one is worthy of the company and the favor [*del commerzio e grazia*] of every great lord" (I, xiv, Maier, pp. 105–6; Singleton, pp. 105–6).

This passage is also interesting for the differing uses that are made of the word grace in the two places where it occurs. At the end of the statement the sense is clearly the same—alluding, that is, to the end or object of the process—as we have seen in the preceding examples. At the beginning, however, the "certa grazia e, come si dice, un sangue," on the one hand seems to consist of an initial quality that determines the desired result ("un sangue, che lo faccia al primo aspetto a chiunque lo vede grato ed amabile"), on the other, it would seem to coincide with the *non so che* described by Wittkower. Yet more precisely, I should say, this grace, coming as it does at the end of a list ("nobiltà, . . . ingegno e bella forma di persona e di volto"), and preceded by a "but" that, rather than opposing, seems to comprehend and color all the preceding qualities, signifies not so much a particular quality as a modality, an ability: the graceful use of qualities to provoke grace ("e questo sia un ornamento che componga e compagni tutte le operazioni sue e prometta . . . quel tale esser degno . . . di grazia"). A modality, thus, rather than a fixed, identifiable quality: here is an important, even fundamental theme that will recur in the treatment of that other grace, which the courtier can and must learn, and more generally of the learning and exercise of his profession, an art that consists, as it has been effectively put by Richard A. Lanham, not in learning "a pattern of concepts, of whatever sort, but a skill."[9] Or, to vary our term somewhat, we may describe it in the Aristotelian sense as a virtue, resulting from habit, become in itself a habit: an habitual state. We can scarcely wonder, therefore, if already at this first level, that of grace which we may define as natural, it is not confused, and even explicitly distinguished from beauty. In chapter xix of Book I, Bibbiena makes a distinction between the "beauty of [his] person," which he doubts, and "the grace of countenance [*la grazia del volto*]" which, as Canossa declares, "you can truly be said to have." "Although the features of it are not very delicate, . . . we do see beyond any doubt that your aspect is very agreeable [*gratissimo*] and pleasant to all"; and he adds that Bibbiena's face "has something manly about it, and yet is full of grace [*grazioso*]" (I, xiv, Maier, p. 114; Singleton, p. 36).

But let us come at last to the other grace. Canossa has already recommended several qualities to be required of an excellent courtier: the use of arms, honor, faith, discretion in praising himself, agility in every physical exercise, wrestling, fencing, horsemanship, and so on. While setting out his requirements he has two or three times included the *caveat* that the courtier must temper "his every action with a certain good judgement and grace [*un certo bon giudicio e grazia*], if he would deserve that universal favor which is so greatly prized" (I, xxi, Maier, p. 118; Singleton, p. 38).[10] At this point Cesare Gonzaga intervenes to request an explanation, or, more precisely, Canossa having "aroused" in his audience "un'ardente sete," an ardent desire to attain this grace, which he has added "as a seasoning without which all the other properties and good qualities would be of little worth" (Singleton, p. 41), Gonzaga now invites him to quench it, to satisfy it with his teaching. It is well to note that Gonzaga, in formulating his request, has reaffirmed the distinction we have observed between those few who possess grace by "a gift of nature and the heavens," and so have no need for teachers, being already "not only pleasing [*grati*], but admirable to everyone," and the many "who are less endowed by nature and are capable of acquiring grace only if they put forth labor, industry, and care." This being the case, "by what art, by what discipline, by what method," can the latter "gain this grace, both in bodily exercises, . . . and in every other thing they do or say [*come in ogni altra cosa che si faccia e dica*]"? (ibid.)

Canossa, being called upon thus peremptorily to extinguish Gonzaga's "ardent thirst," does not excuse himself from the "obligation" put upon him, but characteristically—characteristic, that is, of Castiglione's strategy in the text—before stating the form of his doctrine he offers an example of it, to put grace into practice. Hence he effects a *correctio*, with a gesture that is perhaps analogous to the author's choice for the book of a dialogue or portrait form, in preference to the catechistical form of a treatise. "Obligato non son io," "I am not bound—said the Count—to teach you how to acquire grace or anything else, but only to show you what a perfect Courtier ought to be. . . . So I, perhaps, shall be able to tell you what a perfect Courtier should be, but not to teach you what you must do to become one" (I, xxv, Maier, p. 122; Singleton, pp. 41–42). Canossa's restatement of his charge, including as it does a refusal to take on the ungracious task of teaching grace, has already all the earmarks of *sprezzatura*, of which he is about to speak. In effect, the model to be imitated has already been displayed, but covertly, that is to say without affectation. Now he suggests the mode of imitation, that will be indeed more like assimilation, and will call to mind not so much the ape as the bee. "Therefore, whoever would be a good pupil must not only do things well, but must always make every effort to resemble and, if that be possible, to transform himself into his master. And when he feels that he has made some progress, it is very profitable to observe different men of that profession; and, conducting himself with that good judgment [*bon giudicio*] which must always be his guide, go about choosing now this thing from one and that from another. And even as in green meadows the bee flits about among the grasses robbing the flowers, so our Courtier must steal this grace from those who seem to have it, taking from each the part that seems most worthy of praise; not doing as a friend of ours whom you all know, etc." (I, xxv, Maier, p. 123; Singleton, pp. 42–43).

We cannot doubt that we are dealing here with an art, or rather with a virtue, ἀρετή in the Aristotelian sense, to be apprehended and exercised. And in so far as it is an art, exactly like painting or the art of speaking referred to in another place, Castiglione holds the observation and imitation of existing models, the best possible models, to be essential to it. In his dedicatory letter to Don Michel de Silva, Bishop of Viseo, Castiglione, pronouncing himself in favor of *lingua cortegiana*, proposes to take account of "la consuetudine del parlare," "the idiom of the other noble cities of Italy where men gather who are wise, talented, and eloquent, and who discourse on great matters pertaining to the governing of states, as well as on letters, war, and business" (Maier, p. 74; Singleton, pp. 4–5): a declaration which we may take as a noteworthy, if not definitive, indication of what the "bona consuetudine," "good usage in speech," of chapter xxxv in Book I, can mean.[11] In the light of the letter to Don Michel de Silva, we can say that this language pertains manifestly to a class. It has "grace," it is *grata*. Here, as elsewhere, the question of grace cannot be propounded absolutely, but in relation to at least two coordinates, those answering to these questions: when and for whom? With these two we can, of course, include a third: where? Even if, at times, Castiglione's discussion tends inevitably to exceed the given place (the court), time (the Italy of his day in which he worked and wrote), and class (his own, whose portrait and apology he makes), yet the place, the time, and most especially the class of and for whom he wrote must be continuously borne in mind, if we wish to understand the *Courtier*. For this reason we may find that to refer the *grazia* (or *sprezzatura* or *affettazione*) he speaks of in this context to words and concepts either anterior or posterior—the χάρις of Demetrius of Phalerum or Dionysius of Halicarnassus, for example, or the *venustas* of the Elder Pliny or Quintilian, the *decorum* of Cicero, the *grazia* of Firenzuola, Della Casa, or Vasari, and so forth—will prove more misleading than helpful. Not that the meaning of the word *grazia* in Castiglione is divorced from, or independent of the Greco-Latin tradition: not at all. But it is certainly significant that he was constrained to invent a new word, *sprezzatura*, to express an idea that was not unknown either to the Greeks or to the Latins. Why a new word, then, and why that particular word?

The famous passage in Book I, chapter xxvi, has been quoted a thousand times, but I cannot do so without recalling here, in my turn, its most salient features: "But, having thought many times already about how this grace is acquired (leaving aside those who have it from the stars), I have found quite a universal rule which in this matter seems to me valid above all others, and in all human affairs whether in word or deed" (Maier, p. 124; Singleton, p. 43). At this point the discussion would appear to be maintained on a very general level: "una regola generalissima [quite a universal rule]," "tutte le cose umane che si facciano e dicano [all human affairs whether in word or deed]." It is on the contrary precisely at this moment that the word grace comes to be delimited, and assumes its special meaning for the work. Look at the first, negative prescription: "And that is to avoid affectation in every way possible as though it were some very rough and dangerous reef" (ibid.). Whenever did grace come to consist in the avoiding of affectation? If we wish to make the *venustas* of Pliny and Cicero, or the *gratia* of Quintilian the ancestor of Castiglione's *grazia* and *sprezzatura*, we should also not forget that in Pliny the *nimia diligentia* that cancels χάρις, *venustas*, refers only to art, and more precisely to the painting of Apelles as opposed to that of Protogenes;[12] by the same token in Cicero it is a question of the oratory of Lysias, in which "quaedam etiam neglegentia est diligens," and, just as with women who go "unadorned," yet "pulchriores esse dicuntur," "are said to be more beautiful," so also in the Greek orator "fit enim quiddam . . . quo sit venustius, sed not ut appareat," "there is something . . . which lends greater charm, but without showing itself"; again in Quintilian the reference is once more to Apelles in *Institutio Oratoria*, XII, x, 6, and to Lysias in IX, iv, 17, and then to Horace and Terence.[13] We are still very far from "tutte le cose umane che si facciano o dicano," "all human affairs whether in word or deed."

All the same, if this enormous extension of *grazia*, or rather of the possible areas to which this word is applicable, is real, it is not yet indiscriminate or undetermined. Just who are they that do or say "tutte le cose umane"? On reconsideration it appears that they are almost exclusively the members, actual or potential,[14] of the "club." On the other hand, Castiglione, in describing the making of the courtier as concerned with the search for a certain perfection within the context of a predetermined scope of activity, without making of the book the treatise on human nature that Burckardt could conjure up by citing those of its parts, which perhaps would be more in place in such a treatise, best suited to such an endeavor, nevertheless by restricting his objective to a single class, whose ambition is to lead, in other words not by obscuring but actually by advocating its distinctive ideology, in many respects quite consciously refers back to, and find himself in accord with the most classical ethical formulations, most particularly, as I have indicated, with that of Aristotle. In many respects, indeed, the very aim of this book is $\dot{\alpha}\rho\epsilon\tau\dot{\eta}$, this being made to consist in $\mu\epsilon\sigma\acute{o}\tau\eta s$, the "giusto mezzo," the *mediocritas* referred to several times in the text:[15] that proper mean that in respect to worth is also, as Aristotle describes it, an apex and extreme.[16] And just as in the philosopher, $\dot{\alpha}\rho\epsilon\tau\dot{\eta}$ depends on three factors: nature, habit and science ($\phi\acute{v}\sigma\iota s$, $\ddot{\epsilon}\theta o s$, $\lambda\acute{o}\gamma o s$).[17] We may even perhaps add that the more aristocratic character of the *Courtier* has led the writer to go back and reappropriate elements antecedent to the Aristotelian synthesis itself, as for example the insistence on nobility and the dependence of $\dot{\alpha}\rho\epsilon\tau\dot{\eta}$ on the approbation of the group, and its definition as in Pindar and Theognis, as a successful activity ($\epsilon\dot{v}\pi\rho\alpha\gamma\acute{\iota}\alpha$).

But, we asked, what need is there for a new word, and why that word? Turning back now to Book I, chapter xxvi, we find that Canossa, having described what is to be avoided "in every way possible as though it were some very rough and dangerous reef," affectation, continues: "and (to pronounce a new word perhaps) to practice in all things a certain *sprezzatura*, so as to conceal all art and make whatever is done or said appear to be without effort and almost without any thought about it." What is the novelty of this word, that it should have given such endless trouble to translators? In order to understand it properly, I think we must consider the nature of this disdain, misprision, or depreciation, that the etymology suggests. At the most immediate and evident semantic level, these terms apply to (and qualify) *diligentia*, the very art that is put into operation by the practitioner. Hence comes the oxymoron: an art without art, a negligent diligence, an inattentive attention. The contrary, and enemy of *sprezzatura*, Castiglione tells us plainly, is affectation, that consists in overstepping the "certain limits of moderation [*certi termini di mediocrità*]," wherein resides the "excellence" of *sprezzatura*.

Here we may note the exact repetition of the Aristotelian scheme mentioned above. It will be worthwhile for our purposes, however, to refer more precisely than we have yet done to Book II of the *Nicomachean Ethics*, when the philosopher, turning his attention to those virtues and vices relative to interpersonal relations, identifies the virtue that he calls ἀλήθεια, or truthfulness, as proper measure, its two extremes being on the one hand boastfulness, ἀλαζονεία, and on the other εἰρωνεία, or irony. Both the latter imply προσποίησις, dissimulation, pretence. The difference between them is that while the former goes too far in the direction of excess, ἐπὶ τὸ μεῖζον, whereby a man makes claim to merits he does not possess and inflates those he does, the latter lags too far behind, tending towards paucity, ἐπὶ τὸ ἔλαττον, so that it intentionally diminishes those merits, and takes the form of understatement.[18] Aristotle's attitude towards εἰρωνεία is, however, singular, and, I should say, ambiguous. Though he does not hesitate to condemn ἀλαζονεία, he is extremely cautious with respect to irony. When speaking of magnanimity in Book IV of the *Ethics*, Aristotle repeats his praise of the ἀληθευτικός and αὐθέκαστος, of the truthful and straightforward character which the magnanimous man will evince in all his words and actions, καὶ τῷ βίῳ καί τῷ λόγῳ. His language will be truthful and straightforward, ἀληθευτικός, "unless when he has recourse to irony, which will be his tone in addressing the generality of men."[19] Again in Book IV, chapter vii, part 9, after repeating that both εἴρων and ἀλαζών are insincere and hence blameworthy, he goes on to say that if a frank and truthful man is obliged to deviate from the truth, he should have recourse to understatement in preference to exaggeration: ἐπὶ τὸ ἔλαττον δὲ μᾶλλον τοῦ ἀληθοῦς ἀποκλίνει. And the reason, interestingly enough, that he gives for this preference is that irony would seem to have more grace, it has a more elegant effect, as opposed to the crudity, the distastefulness that must accompany any excess: ἐμμελέστερον γὰρ φαίνεται διὰ τὸ ἐπαχθεῖς τὰς ὑπερβολὰς εἶναι. Once again in IV, vii, 14, we read that ironic persons give an impression of superior refinement: οἱ δ'εἴρωνες ἐπὶ τὸ ἔλαττον λέγοντες χαριέστεροι μὲν τὰ ἤθη φαίνονται, ("because we feel that their way of speaking is not dictated by greed or gain but by the desire to avoid showing off").[20] Thus, if men employ irony in moderation and when the subject is not too banal and obvious, χαρίεντες φαίνονται, they appear to possess distinction, χάρις, and so make a pleasant impression. Here it will be well also to recall the passage in the *Rhetoric* on wit, of which some varieties are deemed appropriate, ἁρμόττει, for use by a gentleman, an ἐλευθέρῳ, but others not.[21] In this context Aristotle affirms that irony is more fitting for a gentleman than buffoonery: ἔστι δ'ἡ εἰρωνεία τῆς βωμολοχίας ἐλευθεριώτερον. In using irony, indeed, he seeks his own amusement; in playing the buffoon that of others.

Why then did Castiglione, who almost certainly was familiar with these passages, choose to ignore the proper mean of Aristotle, which in this case was ἀλήθεια, and, while continuing to speak of "certain limits of moderation," and *mediocritas*, to privilege instead the word corresponding to εἰρωνεία, *sprezzatura*? It may be useful here, if perhaps not entirely necessary after so much has already been said, to repeat with G. C. Sedgewick, the author of a good study, *Of Irony, Especially in Drama*, that, even though the notion of irony "as understatement—a mere rhetorical figure—derives from Aristotle, it was not the centre of his idea of *eironeia*. In the *Ethics eironeia* is a pervasive mode of behaviour, a constant pretence of self-depression, of which understatement is only one manifestation."[22] But again, why did Castiglione abandon the orthodox (I refer to the etymology) ἀλήθεια for the paradox of *sprezzatura*?

The answer, I believe, will be found in a certain sense implicit in some of the observations of Aristotle, and particularly in those, shall we say, embroiled pronouncements on εἰρωνεία, that I have cited above. When he speaks of distinction, of elegance, of finesse, he seems to discover in the use of this word an attitude to class values that we must call aristocratic. We have already particularly noticed how the magnanimous man will have recourse to irony in his dealings with the generality of men, the masses. It might further be interesting to note that traditionally writers treating the subject of irony have dwelt almost exclusively on its polemic as opposed to its playful aim.[23] But in our case, or rather that of Castiglione, against whom is the polemic directed, against whom the misprision, and who is the butt of the joke?

We know that the essential thing for the practice of irony, as also of *sprezzatura*, is dissimulation: a trick, or at any rate always a detachment, a discrepancy between being and seeming. A dissimulation obviously is intended to the disadvantage of someone. Whose, and of what sort is this deception? What are its characteristics and its limits, if limits there are? Let us try to articulate the structure of the communicative process with which we are dealing. The success of irony, as of *sprezzatura*, or as of a witticism, obviously depends on its reception. The public is the arbitrator of grace, that is, of the success or failure of *sprezzatura*. This we know, but what public? Will it be the generality, the mass, or a more restricted, qualified public, the "happy few"? This is the crucial point, but also the least attended to: indeed, to tell the truth, it has been completely ignored in the treatment of this text.

In my opinion it is necessary, in order to understand this process —and the same goes, to a certain extent, for wit as for irony—to postulate a structure that is not simply dyadic (emitter-receiver), but at least triadic. We must therefore admit, in the case in question, a splitting up of the receiver, the public, into two parts, one of which is not necessarily present on the scene. One of these parts will recognize an instance of *sprezzatura* or irony for what it really communicates, and thus sanction its success; the other will take the action or affirmation at its face value, admire, without recognizing, the *sprezzatura* or irony: in other words it will serve as its victim. The price it pays will be its exclusion from the "club" of the "happy few." To put it differently, *sprezzatura* is the test the courtier must pass in order to be admitted to this club, to obtain the recognition of his peers. This division of the public into general and restricted exists above all to remind us that what is at play is a contest for distinction, with the everpresent and actual risk of failure. The enemy, the seeming adversary would be affectation, or exaggeration of any kind. But to combat such an adversary, as Aristotle foresaw, ἀλήθεια would be sufficient. The real enemy of *sprezzatura* is something else again: the lack of *sprezzatura*, the quality of being explicit instead of implicit, direct instead of indirect. *Sprezzatura* functions like a set of inverted commas, that it would be unpardonable to omit. The inverted commas are there, though invisible: for those who have not the skill to see. The appeal of *sprezzatura* is to those who have that skill.

The interpretative scheme I have attempted to set out is no more than that, a scheme, that cannot but simplify a textual reality that is much richer and more complex, and at times, indeed, even contradictory. Yet such as it is the scheme still seems to me to be able to render some account of certain textual difficulties that would otherwise remain inexplicable, and at the same time to distinguish and set in a historical context the grace that is the preoccupation of Castiglione's courtier.

The grace of the courtier, Canossa is made to say, depends on *sprezzatura*: that is on a certain excellence, in itself rare and difficult, that gives the impression of facility. This impression, given the difficulty understood to reside in the attainment of such excellence ("because every one knows the difficulty of things that are rare and well done" [Singleton, p. 43]), provokes wonder and admiration. In whom? At this point it would be fair to say, in the public in general, without distinction of kind. But why must the art be concealed? And what does it signify that it must? "Because if it is discovered, this robs a man of all credit and causes him to be held in slight esteem," is Canossa's answer (ibid.). Here the text follows with an example, in order to demonstrate the validity of this observation. The example itself, however, is problematical, and can be applied to our case, only if we refer it to one part of the public: "And I remember having read of certain most excellent orators in ancient times who, among the other things they did, tried to make everyone believe that they had no knowledge whatever of letters; and dissembling their knowledge, they made their orations appear to be composed in the simplest manner and according to the dictates of nature and truth rather than of effort and art; which fact, had it been known, would have inspired in the minds of the people the fear that they could be duped by it" (Maier, pp. 124–25; Singleton, pp. 43–44).

Here again it is evident that we must distinguish between two levels: between two publics, and also between fiction and reality. Obviously the orations to which Canossa refers must have been very differently received by the members of the public who were to be persuaded, and those in the know: fellow advocates, for instance. The former are deceived in earnest (it is not the question here whether this deception be to a good end); the latter will admire the art of the orator, and in him recognize an excellent compeer. But what if this artifice were evident, or were exposed? The result would be doubly catastrophic. The first public would recognize the trick, and refuse to let itself be persuaded; the other would moreover find deplorable (affected, inelegant, strained, perhaps even unprofessional) the performance of their colleague. For this restricted public of the competent, *sprezzatura* consists, beyond doubt, of a performance, like a conjuring act, which they attend, knowing full well that there is some trick: there must be, even if they cannot find it out. The other public does not even guess that there is a trick. Its wonder may seem alike, but it is not: it belongs, in effect, to a completely different order. The ideal, then, is "that pure and charming simplicity which is so appealing [*grata*] to all" (Maier, p. 127; Singleton, p. 45): but the group in the know are well aware that they must take the word in inverted commas, that their "simplicity" and "nature" are artificial constructions.

If we go a little further, in chapter xxviii, we find that Canossa adds a significant codicil: "Thus, this excellence (which is opposed to affectation, and which, at the moment, we are calling *sprezzatura*), besides being the real source from which grace springs, brings with it another adornment which, when it accompanies any human action however small, not only reveals at once how much the person knows who does it, but often causes it to be judged much greater than it actually is, since it impresses upon the minds of the onlookers the opinion that he who performs well with so much facility must possess even greater skill than this, and that, if he were to devote care and effort to what he does, he could do it far better" (Maier, p. 128; Singleton, p. 46). Who are these "onlookers"? To which public does this refer? Without doubt to the general, rather than the restricted. The latter know perfectly well that the result they witness implies "care and effort." *Sprezzatura*, that results in grace—as indeed every other worthy activity of man—derives from the so-called "giudicio naturale" (Maier, p. 163) or "bon giudicio" (Maier, p. 163), that is by no means natural, or solely natural, but is also the fruit of education, experience, and reason. Above all, it is the index of the courtier's preoccupation with his social image, or, to be more precise, his "grado," his rank, and the dignity and distinction inherent there.

Take the problem raised in chapters ix and x of Book II, whether it is suitable for a gentleman to participate in "a country festival . . . where the spectators and the company were persons of low birth" (Maier, p. 203; Singleton, p. 101). Federico Fregoso is of the negative opinion, and if at the end he concedes such activities to the courtier, it is only with the greatest caution and, in particular, as regards dancing or partaking in "public spectacles, either armed or unarmed" (Maier, p. 206; Singleton, p. 103), only if he adopt a disguise: "but not in public, unless he is masquerading [*fuor che travestito*], for then it is not unseemly even if he should be recognized by all. . . . Because masquerading [*lo esser travestito*] carries with it a certain freedom and license, which among other things enables one to choose the role in which he feels most able, and to bring diligence and a care for elegance into that principal aim, and to show a certain *sprezzatura* in what does not matter: all of which adds much charm [*accresce molto la grazia*]; as for a youth to dress as a rustic shepherd, or in some other such costume, but astride a perfect horse and gracefully attired in character: because the bystanders immediately take in what meets the eye at first glance; whereupon, realizing that here there is much more than was promised by the costume, they are delighted and amused [*si diletta e piglia piacere*]" (Maier, p. 206; Singleton, p. 103).

Even in this instance it is ostensibly a question of *sprezzatura* and *grazia*. But here the detachment between being and seeming introduced by the use of disguise functions in a manner different from our previous examples. Now clearly the public is homogenous, not divided; it is the general public, or, to be precise, a public socially inferior to the actor. The disguise functions very much as the inverted commas, but visible to all: or rather, they gradually become apparent to all. The structure of this process is no longer, however, that of irony or *sprezzatura*, as we have outlined it in the preceding discussion. Despite the distinction developed by some theorists between covert and overt irony, and the attempt of Alcanter de Brahm—an attempt deservedly doomed to failure—to introduce a novel form of punctuation, "le petit signe flagellateur,"[24] in order to eliminate the ambiguity of irony, I believe that it was the character of Hans Castorp rather than that of the optimist Settembrini from *The Magic Mountain*, who was right when he asked himself, before the prospect of an unequivocable irony: what kind of irony is that anyway? The rhetorical structure of the process described in these last passages from the *Courtier* might better be classed with that of allegory, just because it unfolds in time and requires a period of unravelling. True *sprezzatura*, it seems to me, like irony, or wit, requires not the passage of time, but instantaneousness.

The dissimulation of *sprezzatura*, like that of irony, is ambiguous and equivocal, nor can it be otherwise,[25] and any attempt to circumscribe its dangerous possibilities would be in vain. As Friedrich Schlegel wrote of irony, one does not play, "one absolutely must not play"[26] with irony. It is a weapon, doubtless, and double-edged; and its use, though rhetorical, does not therefore pertain any less to reality. What the courtier is playing at is no game, or if it is, it is like that of the trapeze artist, who plays without the net. There are no inverted commas to catch him, to keep him safe from disastrous slips.

Besides, as in any other communicative process, there are no rules or recipes to guarantee success. The actor must possess "prudenza," "discrezione," and "bon giudicio" ("prudence," "discretion," and "good judgement") (Maier, pp. 197–98; Singleton, pp. 96–97). But for the performance to be a success, prudence, discretion, and good judgement must also belong in the public for whom the spectacle is destined.

Translated by Susan G. Beecher

NOTES

1. Eugenio Garin, *L'Umanesimo italiano* (Bari: Universale Laterza, 1964), p. 137.
2. Rudolph Wittkower, "Genius: Individualism in Art and Artists," in Philip P. Wiener, ed., *Dictionary of the History of Ideas* (New York: Charles Scribner's Sons, 1973), 2: 304.
3. Samuel Holt Monk, "A Grace beyond the Reach of Art," *Journal of the History of Ideas* 5, no. 2 (April 1944): 131–50.
4. Sir Anthony Blunt, *Artistic Theory in Italy, 1450–1600* (Oxford: Clarendon, Press, 1940), pp. 97–98.
5. *Thesaurus Linguae Latinae*, vol. 6 (Leipzig: B. G. Teubner, 1934). An exhaustive study on *gratia* and its family is that of Claude Moussy, *Gratia et sa famille* (Paris: Presses Universitaires de France, 1966). It is interesting from our perspective to read there that "le sens de la majorité des dérivés de [la] racine [*g^wer-(∂^2)] se rattache à celui de 'louange' " (p. 35); also that "un des caractères essentiels de cette louange est qu'elle n'est pas désintéressée et, comme l'exprime bien la formule proposée par G. Dumézil: *laudo ut des* [cf. *Servius et la fortune*, p. 89], qu'elle contraint en quelque sorte celui à qui elle s'adresse à répondre par des bienfaits" (p. 37). We may further learn that the variety of semantic fields in which words from this family, and *grātia* in particular, can be found (from religion to justice, gratitude, friendship, politics and aesthetics) is not as dispersive as it appears to be. "Les différents significations prises par *grātia* ont toutes un lien entre elles: toutes se rattachent d'une façon ou d'une autre à la pratique de la bienfaisance, toutes s'expliquent à partir des sens fondamentaux de 'reconnaissance' et de 'paiement en retour'. L'extension des valeurs de la famille de *grātia* depuis la sphère religieuse jusqu'aux domaines moral, social, politique peut se schématiser ainsi: cette famille de mots a servi d'abord à exprimer les relations entre les hommes et les dieux, puis les relations des hommes entre eux, relations dont on peut affirmer dans les deux cas, sans vouloir restreindre la religion des Romains à la pratique du *do ut des*, qu'elles sont fondées essentiellements sur le couple que constituent le bienfait et la reconnaissance" (p. 475). As for the seeming contradiction between an expression like *grātiam referre*, for instance, and words like *grātiīs, grātuītus, grātuītō*, one must consider, as Moussy rightly points out, that for Roman law the two notions of gratuitousness and remuneration are not "antonymes, mais solidaires; toutes deux se fondent sur la réprocité: le don gratuit, comme toute autre presta-

tion, appelle une compensation, un contre-don. (On the obligatory character of this exchanges, which in archaic societies was certainly more evident than in Roman society, see E. Benveniste, "Don et échange dans le vocabulaire indo-européen," *Année Sociologique*, 3d ser., 1948–1949, pp. 7–20, and M. Mauss, "Essai sur le don, form archaique de l'échange," *Année Sociologique*, n.s. 1, 1923–1924).

Finally, even if it is certainly true that the Greek χάρις is behind the two meanings late to develop of the word *gratia*, that is the aesthetic and the Christian, there is nothing surprising in this development: "les mots de la famille de *grātia* sont souvent joints à des termes qui expriment la joie, et servent parfois eux-mêmes à l'expression de la joie:" and "l'association de la joie et de la reconnaissance est on ne peut plus naturelle dans les paroles, comme dans l'âme, de qui a vu exaucer ses voeux" (p. 480). More specifically, for Christian *grātia*: "Outre son équivalence avec χάρις, et ses valeurs anciennes de 'faveur', de 'bienfait', ce qui prédestinait en quelque sorte le mot à devenir le nom latin du 'don gratuit' qu'est la grâce de Dieu, c'est avant tout que l'expression de la gratuité était étroitment liée à la famille de *grātia*" (ibid.).

6. References within the text are to Maier's edition of *Il libro del Cortegiano con una scelta delle opere minori di B.C.*, a cura di Bruno Maier, second edition (Turin: U.T.E.T., 1964), and to Charles S. Singleton's translation of *The Book of the Courtier*, a new translation by C.S.S. (Garden City, N.Y.: Anchor Books, Doubleday & Co., 1959).

7. "But, to return to our subject, I say that there is a mean to be found between such supreme grace on the one hand and such stupid ineptitude on the other, and that those who are not so perfectly endowed by nature can, with care and effort, polish and in great part correct their natural defects" (Singleton, p. 29).

8. This is obviously restricted to the aristocratic class, of which the prince himself is a part. Hence the book's insistence—required by the logic of the argument —on the perequisite for the courtier of a noble birth, for him to be born in a "nobile e generosa famiglia" (I, xiv, p. 103).

9. Cf. Richard A. Lanham, *The Motives of Eloquence: Literary Rhetoric in the Renaissance* (New Haven: Yale University Press, 1976), p. 149. "Reading *The Courtier* is like learning to ride a bicycle, not like learning about Renaissance Platonism." What follows, however, is less convincing: "So, here, Castiglione tries to teach us a skill, an intuitive not a conscious, considered response."

10. And in I, xxii: "If such agility is accompanied by grace, in my opinion it makes a finer show than any other;" and also "let him do all that others do, yet never depart from comely conduct [*dai laudevoli atti*], but behave himself with that good judgement [*bon giudicio*] which will not allow him to engage in any folly; let him laugh, jest, banter, frolic, and dance, yet in such a manner as to show always that he is genial and discreet [*ingenioso e discreto*]; and let him be full of grace [*aggraziato*] in all that he does or says" (Singleton, p. 39).

11. In I, xxxv, class qualification may seem to be absent, while it is actually only less explicit. Canossa states there in a more general way that "good usage in speech . . . springs from men who have talent, and who through learning and experience [*dottrina ed esperienzia*] have attained good judgement [*il bon giudicio*]" (Maier, p. 144; Singleton, p. 58). But note that the latter, deriving from "dottrina

ed esperienzia," is immediately and equivocally, it would seem, redefined as follows: "and who thereby [*con quello*, i.e., *il bon giudicio*] agree among themselves and consent to adopt those words which to them seem good; which words are recognized by virtue or a certain natural judgement and not by any art or rule" (ibid.). "Natural," however, must be understood as "diventato naturale," "that has become natural," if it is a product of doctrine and experience. The same should be said of Canossa's polemic against "grammatical rules," to which "figures of speech" (*le figure del parlare*) are opposed, consisting precisely of "abusioni" ("abuses of grammatical rules."). These are said to "give so much grace and luster to discourse [*grazia e splendor alla orazione*]," but only if "accepted and confirmed by usage," this being qualified obviously as above. The polemic here is clearly directed against absolute and metaphysical values, in the name and favor of history and usage: of uses and conventions which are historical.

12. C. Plinii Secundi *Nat. Hist.* XXXV, 79–80, in K. Jex-Blake and E. Sellers, eds., *The Elder Pliny Chapters on the History of Art* (Chicago: Ares Publishers, 1976), p. 120.

13. M. Tulli Ciceronis *Ad M. Brutum Orator*, ed. John E. Sandys (Cambridge: At the University Press, 1885), pp. 89–90; M. Fabio Quintiliano, *L'Istituzione Oratoria*, Latin text and Italian translation edited by R. Faranda (Turin: U.T.E.T., 1968), 2: 678, 336.

14. Illustrious people from antiquity, and artists, ancient and modern, are clearly to be included among the potential members of this club. Their excellence is obviously responsible of their inclusion in both cases. A further distinction ought perhaps to be made, within the second group, between literary men and other artists. It seems certain, at any rate, that in Giovan Cristoforo Romano's case, for instance, his opinion is asked for only in matters concerning his profession. On the other hand, if Bembo is given such a prominent part to play in the book, one cannot forget that the literary man was also a Venetian nobleman.

15. A "certain decorous mean" (*certa onesta mediocrità*) is mentioned for instance in II, xli, while talking of the courtier; a "certain mean, difficult to achieve and, as it were, composed of contraries" (*certa mediocrità difficile e quasi composta di cose contrarie*) in III, v, while speaking of the Court Lady (Maier, pp. 254, 343; Singleton, pp. 139, 207).

16. *Eth. Nic.* II, vi, 17–18; "Thus, looked at from the point of view of its essence, . . . virtue no doubt is a mean; judged by the standard of what is right and best, it is an extreme" (J. A. K. Thomson's translation, in Aristotle, *Ethics*, Penguin Classics, 1955, pp. 66–67). "Διὸ κατὰ μὲν τὴν οὐσίαν καὶ τὸν λόγον τὸν τί, ἦν εἶναι λέγοντα μεσότης ἐστίν, κατὰ δὲ τὸ ἄριστον καὶ τὸ εὖ ἀκρότης."

In *The Ethics of Aristotle, illustrated with essays and notes* by Sir Alexander Grant (London: Longmans, Green, and Co., 1874), 1: 499–500.

17. *Pol.* VII, xiiii, 39–40; *Eth. Nic.* X, x, 20–21.

18. *Eth. Nic.* II, vii, 12: "Well then, as regards veracity [το ἀληθές], the character who aims at the mean [μέσος] may be called 'truthful' [ἀληθής] and what he aims at 'truthfulness [ἀλήθεια]. Pretending [προσποίησις] when it goes too far [ἐπὶ το μεῖζον] is 'boastfulness' [ἀλαζονεία] and the man who shows it is a 'boaster' or 'braggart' [ἀλαζών]. If it takes the form of understatement [ἐπὶ το ἔλαττον], the pretence

is called 'irony' [εἰρωνεία] and the man who shows it 'ironical' [εἴρων]. (In Thompson's translation, p. 70).

19. *Eth. Nic.* IV, iii, 28: "πλὴν ὅσα μὴ δι' εἰρωνείαν. εἴρωνα δὲ πρὸς τοὺς πολλούς."

20. Thompson, p. 132.

21. *Rhet.* III, 18, 1419ᵇ, 6–9: "ὧν τὸ μὲν ἁρμόττει ἐλευθέρῳ τὸ δ'οὔ. ὅπως οὖν τὸ ἁρμόττον αὑτῷ λήψεται. ἔστι δ'ἡ εἰρωνεία τῆς βωμολοχίας ἐλευθεριώτερον. ὁ μὲν γὰρ αὑτοῦ ἕνεκα ποιεῖ τὸ γελοῖον, ὁ δὲ βωμολόχος ἑτέρου." Aristotelis *Ars Rhetorica*, ed. Rudolf Kassel (Berlin: Walter De Gruyter, 1976), p. 196.

22. G. C. Sedgewick, *Of Irony, Especially in Drama* (Toronto: University of Toronto Press, 1935), p. 10. With this in mind, we may feel less surprised at Daniel Javitch's recent reminder, in his excellent *Poetry and Courtliness in Renaissance England* (Princeton: Princeton University Press, 1978), that authors like George Puttenham and Fulke Greville recognized in Castiglione's courtier's behavior an affinity, if not an identity, with the procedures of classical rhetoric, in particular with that of irony.

23. Cf. Antonino Pagliaro, *Ironia e verità* (Milano: Rizzoli editore, 1970), pp. 14–15.

24. Cf. Douglas C. Muecke, *The Compass of Irony* (London: Methuen, 1969), p. 56.

25. On this in particular see the discussion between Gaspare Pallavicino and Federico Fregoso in II, 40.

26. "Über die Unverständlichkeit," *Kritische Ausgabe* (Zurich: Verlag Ferdinand Schöningh, 1967), 2: 369: "Mit der Ironie ist durchaus nicht zu scherzen."

THREE

ARATEAN CROSSTICS: PLEXED ARTISTRY

William Levitan

> φύσις κρύπτεσθαι φιλεῖ
> Heraclitus

> Well, we have frankly enjoyed
> more than anything these
> secret workings of nature. . . .
> *Finnegans Wake*

THE AESTHETIC revolution that gave rise to the literature of the Hellenistic period (and ultimately to the literature of Rome) was occasioned at least in part by the growing awareness that the medium of literary expression had suffered a change in orientation from spoken to written language, and that the new emphasis on the visual aspect of literature had opened new possibilities and made new demands on both the writer and his audience. The most dramatic evidence of this re-orientation can be found in a number of figurative poems in the shape of wings, an egg, an altar, an axe, the so-called *technopaegnia* conveniently assembled at the end of Gow's edition of the *Bucolici Graeci*;[1] but its most subtle and revealing manifestation, I think, is in the acrostics of Aratus of Soli.

Despite the prestige and influence of his work in antiquity, Aratus (fl. 270 B.C.) has all but disappeared from the ranks of familiar classical authors. Even among classicists his most important poem, the *Phaenomena*, is not as much read as it is known by its traces—translations into Latin by Cicero and Germanicus Caesar among others, quotation and paraphrase by centuries of ancient writers, pre-eminently Vergil. Ovid's prophecy, then, is today better known than its subject: "cum sole et luna semper Aratus erit."[2] Though disappointing, this is not altogether surprising. Hellenistic literature in general discourages a wide audience. Its elegant, allusive texture, dense and often difficult, does not easily lend itself to the attractive translation that is essential today for any but the smallest readership.[3] And, when the poems themselves make explicit statements of aesthetic value, the recurring expressions of purity, delicacy, restriction, and refinement betoken a literature exclusive by design as well. In this Aratus is an author typically Hellenistic.

The *Phaenomena* (*Starry Sphere* or literally—and more appropriately—*Appearances*) is a didactic poem of less than twelve hundred lines on the subject of natural signs. Its greater part (lines 19–732) is an analytical description of the heavens that closely follows a prose treatise of one of the most famous early astronomers and mathematicians, Eudoxus, a pupil of Plato. Aratus's poem, however, is not a Platonic work but is thought to reflect Stoic influence. A second section, often considered separately as the "Diosemiai" or "Weather-Signs," discusses the meteorological significance of atmospheric, terrestrial, and even biological events; the whole poem becoming thereby a kind of grand semiological compendium.

The *Phaenomena* was designed for manuscript and, more, conceived in terms of a matrix particularly appropriate to a papyrus roll: a rough rectangle of text, its horizontal dimension proceeding from an axis at the left-hand margin to the right for a length determined by the individual hexameter line, its vertical dimension proceeding from top to bottom for a length determined by the column of text on the roll—the prototype, simply, of the ordinary modern page. Such a matrix, of course, facilitates the introduction of acrostics but is not necessarily dominant in an acrostic poem: Gow includes in his collection, for example, one poem in the shape of an altar that is the product of two interfering matrices, one which uses a central axis to make the figure apparent, a second which yields an acrostic.[4] In the case of the *Phaenomena* this rectangular matrix facilitated the introduction of three acrostics.

Plexed Artistry: Aratean Acrostics

The first, rediscovered by J.-M. Jacques,[5] occurs at lines 783–787:

ΛΕΠΤΗ μὲν καθαρή τε περὶ τρίτον ἦμαρ ἐοῦσα
Εὔδιός κ'εἴη· λεπτὴ δὲ καὶ εὖ μάλ'ἐρευθὴς
Πνευματίη· παχίων δὲ καὶ ἀμβλείῃσι κεραίαις
Τέτρατον ἐκ τριτάτοιο φόως ἀμενηνὸν ἔχουσα
Η νότῳ ἄμβλυνται ἢ ὕδατος ἐγγὺς ἐόντος.

[(If the moon's crescent is) slender and clear on the third day, it means fair weather; if slender and with a red cast, wind; if thick and faint on the third and fourth day, then her horns are blunted by a south wind or rain.]

Jacques understands the acrostic here as a reminiscence of word play imagined in the first lines of *Iliad* 24 whose initial letters spell λευκή ("white"):

Λῦτο δ'ἀγών, λαοὶ δὲ θοὰς ἐπὶ νῆας ἕκαστοι
Εσκίδναντ' ἰέναι· τοὶ μὲν δόρποιο μέδοντο
Υπνου τε γλυκεροῦ ταρπήμεναι· αὐτὰρ Ἀχιλλεὺς
Κλαῖε φίλου ἐτάρου μεμνημένος, οὐδέ μιν ὕπνος
Ηρει πανδαμάτωρ, ἀλλ' ἐστρέφετ' ἔνθα καὶ ἔνθα.

The Homeric acrostic must be fortuitous; Hellenistic scholars, however, themselves living comfortably with manuscripts and producing manuscript editions of earlier poets (Aratus is known to have edited the Odyssey), in many ways projected manuscript conventions onto Homer. But Jacques also points out that the key to Aratus's acrostic, the word λεπτή ("subtle, slender, slight") is a term of value particularly important for Hellenistic aesthetics:[6] here is both a bow to Homer and an assertion of modernity.

As far as I know, there is no Homeric inspiration for the other two acrostics. The passage containing both begins at line 802:

πάντη γὰρ καθαρῇ κε μάλ'εὔδια τεκμήραιο·
ΠΑΝΤΑ δ'ἐρευθομένῃ δοκέειν ἀνέμοιο κελεύθους·
Αλλοθι δ'ἄλλο μελαινομένῃ δοκέειν ὑετοῖο.
Σήματα δ'οὐ μάλα πᾶσιν ἐπ'ἤμασι πάντα τέτυκται·
Αλλ'ὅσα μὲν τριτάτῃ τε τεταρταίῃ τε πέλονται,
μέσφα διχαιομένης, διχάδος γε μὲν ἄρχις ἐπ'αὐτὴν
ΣΗΜΑΙΝΕΙ διχόμηνον, ἀτὰρ πάλιν ἐκ διχομήνου
Ες διχάδα φθιμένην· ἔχεται δέ οἱ αὐτίκα τετρὰς

Μηνὸς ἀποιχομένου, τῇ δὲ τριτάτῃ ἐπιόντος.
ΕΙ δέ κέ μιν περὶ πᾶσαν ἁλωαὶ κυκλώσωνται
Η τρεῖς ἠὲ δύω περικείμεναι ἠὲ μί'οἴη. . . .

[When the moon is entirely clear, forecast fair weather; when red over all, wind; when spotted, rain. The signs are not all for each separate day: but the signs of the third and fourth day show the weather up to the half moon; those of the half moon up to midmonth; those of midmonth up to the waning half moon; the signs of the fourth-to-last day follow those of the waning half moon, followed in turn by those of the third day of the new month. If halos encircle the whole moon, triple or double or even one set alone. . . .]

The acrostic beginning at 803 departs somewhat from the earlier model. Instead of being repeated in identical form down the left-hand margin, the key word πάντα ("all") is reflected by its grammatical variants, first by πᾶς the masculine form of the adjective and then, as the initial alpha of the next line is considered, by its feminine form πᾶσα; the adverb πάντη beginning line 802 introduces and, with πᾶσιν and πάντα in 805, augments the sophisticated pattern. Using one of the poem's most important words with unabashed precision—ringing the changes on "all"—this complex rhetorical figure, polyptoton in two dimensions, expresses in grammatical terms one of the poem's important concepts, plenitude and perfection. Compare, for example, the poem's opening lines:

Ἐκ Διὸς ἀρχώμεσθα, τὸν οὐδέποτ'ἄνδρες ἐῶμεν
ἄρρητον· μεσταὶ δὲ Διὸς πᾶσαι μὲν ἀγυιαί,
πᾶσαι δ'ἀνθρώπων ἀγοραί, μεστὴ δὲ θάλασσα
καὶ λιμένες· πάντη δὲ Διὸς κεχρήμεθα πάντες.

[Let us begin with Zeus whom we men never leave unnamed: all the streets are filled with Zeus, and all the market places of men; the sea is filled and the harbors. In all ways do we all have need of Zeus.]

The third acrostic also plays on an important concept, perhaps the most crucial idea of the poem, the idea of signification; and also departs from the simpler acrostic model, here more dramatically. The key word σημαίνει ("to show by a sign, to mean") in line 808, suffers a change in the acrostic from a verb form to the plural noun σημεῖα ("tokens, signs, constellations"); and the acrostic is incomplete, or if complete, misspelled, teetering on the verge of nonsense. At this point in the poem, at least, the reader cannot remain passive: the signs are there to be deciphered.

Plexed Artistry: Aratean Acrostics

I realize that such a brief account alone is insufficient to dispel the uncomfortable feelings the notion of a misspelled acrostic can excite; and further discussion is certainly called for.

Aratus's may not be the only distorted acrostic in Hellenistic literature. Some years ago, E. Lobel published a piece that should become a model for classical articles: it is three sentences long, the first two being introductory, and is worth quoting in full.

It is unusual for Greek poets to sign their work. Nicander ends the *Theriaca* καί κεν 'Ομηρείοιο καὶ εἰσέτι Νικάνδροιο μνῆστιν ἔχοις, and the *Alexipharmaca* καί κ'ἔνθ' ὑμνοπόλοιο καὶ εἰσέτι Νικάνδροιο μνῆστιν ἔχοις. In addition, he embeds his name in the body of his verses; in the *Alexipharmaca* at 11. 266–274:

σ ὺν δὲ καὶ ἀμπελόεις ἕλικας ἐνθρύπτεο νύμφαις
Ι σως καὶ βατόεντα περὶ πορθεῖα κολούσας.
Κ αί τε σὺ γυμνώσειας εὐτρεφέος νέα τέρφη
κ αστηνοῦ, καρύοιο λαχυφλοίοιο κάλυμμα,
Ν είαιραν τόθι σάρκα περὶ σκύλος αὖον ὀπάζει
Δ υσλεπέος καρύοιο, τὸ Κασταν ὶς ἔτρεφεν αἶα.
Ρ εῖα δὲ νάρθηκος νεάτην ἐξαίνυσο νηδύν,
Ο s τε Προμηθείοιο κλοπὴν ἀνεδέξατο φώρης.
Σ ὺν δὲ καὶ ἑρπύλλοιο φιλοζώοιο πέτηλα,

though one can imagine the heat with which this conclusion would have been contested, if at *Theriaca* 345–353,

Ν ειμάμενος κασίεσσιν ἑκὰς περικυδέας ἀρχὰς
Ι δμοσύνηι νεότητα γέρας πόρεν ἡμερίοισι
Κ υδαίνων· δὴ γάρ ῥα πυρὸς ληίστορ' ἔνιπτον
Α φρονες· οὐ γὰρ τῆς γε κακοφραδίης ἀπόνητο.
Ν ωθεῖς γὰρ κάμνοντες ἀμορβεύοντο λεπάργωι
Δ ῶρα· πολύσκαρθμος δὲ κεκαυμένος αὐχενα δίψηι
Ρ ώετο· γωλειοῖσι δ'ἰδὼν ὀλκήρεα θῆρα
Ο ὐλοὸν ἐλλιτάνευε κακῆι ἐπαλαλκέμεν ἄτηι
Σ αίνων· αὐτὰρ ὁ βρῖθος, ὃ δὴ ῥ'ἀνεδέξατο νώτοις,

he had not had better luck.[7]

Surely Lobel is not serious in ascribing the distorted acrostic in the *Alexipharmaca* to bad luck: acrostics, easy enough to produce in English, are easier still in an inflected language like Greek whose word order is much more fluid. But if it is the result of design, as I believe it is, it is an exceptionally curious design. There have been attempts to cushion the shock. An easy emendation has been proposed, νῦν δὲ καὶ in the first line,[8] that would restore the initial letter of Νικανδρος and make the acrostic easier to recognize but without completely addressing the problem in the passage. More helpful is the suggestion of E. L. Brown[9] that the missing alpha in Nicander's name has become redundant, following as it does the initial kappa in the third line of the acrostic—καί—and so insistently in the fourth—καστηνοῦ, καρύοιο, κάλυμμα. Aratus also exploits the initial syllable of a word for an acrostic (in line 811) and Brown points out instances of this procedure in other poems.[10] This suggestion saves Nicander from the charge of bad spelling and dismisses the imputation of bad luck, but still it avoids the central question. If it is presumed that a poet has the means to do what he likes in his poem, what kind of acrostic is a distorted acrostic? What kind of pattern is a broken pattern? What kind of success is there in the near miss? What kind of game is it that obscures its own rules?

This at least is familiar ground. While the type of word play exemplified by the acrostic, the treatment of words as plastic objects, is perhaps yet to emerge as a central theme in twentieth-century writing—the return of the concrete poem is but one indication—, the revival of concern with games in literature and with literature itself as game is certainly widespread.[11] Many readers (and I emphatically include myself), though, are somewhat at a loss to appreciate the *frisson* of joy that mathematicians and a growing number of writers find in word play; but there is no difficulty in finding a modern master of literary gamesmanship who may help us articulate the subtleties of such pleasure and put us in a better position to intuit the sensibility behind the near miss.

You will recall an episode in *Pale Fire*: John Shade—nominal author of the 999 verses that begin the novel—John Shade, obsessed throughout most of his life, but particularly since the suicide of his daughter, with thoughts of death and the riddle of an after-life, suffers a cardiac arrest. During his collapse, which he understands without question as his death, he has a distinct vision of a tall white fountain. He is revived and naturally continues to be fascinated with this clue until he reads a magazine interview with a woman he calls Mrs. Z. whose heart had stopped on the operating table and like Shade had been revived. Like Shade too, she saw a tall white fountain—confirmation! He visits the woman but finds her personally so repulsive that he cannot bear to risk the intimacy a direct question and confession

Plexed Artistry: Aratean Acrostics

would imply; so he leaves her and goes to speak with the journalist who wrote the original interview.

> He took his article from a steel file:
> "It's accurate. I have not changed her style.
> There's one misprint—not that it matters much:
> *Mountain*, not *fountain*. The majestic touch!"
>
> Life Everlasting—based on a misprint!
> I mused as I drove homeward: take the hint,
> And stop investigating my abyss?
> But all at once it dawned on me that *this*
> Was the real point, the contrapuntal theme;
> Just this: not text, but texture; not the dream
> But topsy-turvical coincidence,
> Not flimsy nonsense, but a web of sense.
> Yes! It sufficed that I in life could find
> Some kind of link-and-bobolink, some kind
> Of correlated pattern in the game,
> Plexed artistry, and something of the same
>
> Pleasure in it as they who played it found.
> It did not matter who they were. No sound,
> No furtive light came from their involute
> Abode, but there they were, aloof and mute,
> Playing a game of worlds, promoting pawns
> To ivory unicorns and ebon fauns;
> Kindling a long life here, extinguishing
> A short one there; killing a Balkan king;
> Causing a chunk of ice formed on a high-
> Flying airplane to plummet from the sky
> And strike a farmer dead; hiding my keys,
> Glasses or pipe. Coordinating these
> Events and objects with remote events
> And vanished objects. Making ornaments
> Of accidents and possibilities.[12]

We have to be careful how seriously we can take this insight; after all it is Nabokov I've been quoting, and the fictional Shade himself withdraws from this certainty a few lines later in the poem. But the passage does, I think, shed light on our problem. The near miss as confirmation, as evidence, dim but irrefutable, that a whole pattern of sense does exist; a secret sign to those with a private longing for coherence: now they see as through a glass, darkly, but they do see, excited witnesses present at the moment when design, trembling, just emerges from chaos. The sensibility of the near miss is not everyone's:

procul, O procul este, profani. It is the joy of hermeneutics and by nature esoteric, aristocratic in a way, even mandarin. The connoisseur of its delicate delights avoids the straightforward with the same energy John Shade displays leaving Mrs. Z., and for the same reason, loathing of vulgarity. The pleasure is not in bright lights but the subtle iridescence of sense and nonsense. Obliquity, esotericism, and at all costs nothing vulgar: these may not be, should not be our terms, but they are Nabokov's and they are the Hellenistics'.

Nabokov, curiously, has found his way into the mainstream of modern literature (or perhaps, curiouser, the mainstream has found him.) There is a literary enterprise, however, more marginal than Nabokov's that is in some ways closer to the Hellenistic sensibility, the work of the *Ouvroir de Littérature Potentielle, OuLiPo,* the Paris-based society that has devoted itself to sophisticated and serious word play.[13] *OuLiPo* continues the ancient traditions of word play, the acrostic, the anagram, the palindrome (one was produced of over 5,000 letters),[14] the snowball sentence, bilingual puns, etc.; and it invents new modes. One book by the society's cofounder, the late Raymond Queneau, that has received some notoriety consists of ten sonnets, each sliced into strips, one verse per strip, so that the reader can turn the strips instead of pages and find himself confronted, if he has (literally) nearly infinite patience, with 10^{14} sonnets, all making sense: the book is called *One Hundred Thousand Billion Poems.*[15] An experiment I find especially intriguing involves the transformation of a text by replacing its words with their dictionary definitions, transforming the new text in the same manner, and again *ad lib*. What results plainly is on the threshold of nonsense though by the rules, algebraic if not linguistic, the semantic integrity of the text has not been lost: there is method in the madness if you know where and how to look for it. A group of similar projects takes all the words of one part of speech in a familiar text and replaces them with others of the same part of speech chosen according to some specified rule: each noun, for example, replaced by the noun that comes seventh after it in the dictionary, or the first noun of a text replaced by the last, the second by the next-to-last, and so on.[16] Again, sense is tortured but never obliterated because the system of syntax is preserved. In fact behind this playing tag with chaos lies the presupposition, the necessary presupposition of system, of an order total and finely articulated: not only the iron rules of the game but the larger systems as well—logical, algebraic, linguistic—in which there is consummate sense. The gamesmen of *OuLiPo* are not precisely seekers after meaning like John Shade. They are more like his enigmatic gods, the remote imps who control the world, making ornament—κόσμος—of possibilities, and hiding the keys. Once privy to their secret methods, we can see against the strange darkness of their results the twinkle of grand cohesion. This is what the gamesmen of *OuLiPo* and all literary gamesmen, I think, savor: the sensibility of the near miss is, from a different perspective, the sensibility of total coherence.

Belief in the web of sense, that the universe is in fact thoroughly designed is, of course, widespread and multifarious. It is, for example, the scientist's faith and the sorcerer's. Clinically, it has been called paranoia, as readers of Thomas Pynchon know and more than one visitor to Thomas Jefferson's Monticello have suspected. Religiously, philosophically, it has many names, not the least apt of which is Stoicism, generally considered to be the intellectual matrix of Aratus's *Phaenomena*. But the approach to the sensibility of total coherence has to be different for those of us whose trust in the order of the universe is limited by the suspicion that while the cotillion of neutrinos, pi-mesons, and Joycean quarks, charmed or otherwise, may dance its spastic dance to the sweetest of rhythms—the Heisenberg Fling?—it still will never sing the song of human passion. Points on a graph, like stars in the sky, may be fixed; a bit of the curve that connects them may be sketched or an asterism identified; but the equation that describes the whole curve we expect will remain unknown, the great constellation unnamed.

For many of us, attempts to map the universe inevitably fail. Art can offer momentary illumination, a tentative pattern; and this is not trivial: we all know of books of great scope and importance that are very satisfying and true by any sensible criterion—the *Iliad*, to name only the greatest and truest. But this is not all we can expect:

> cum canerem reges et proelia, Cynthius aurem
> vellit et admonuit, "pastorem, Tityre, pingues
> pascere oportet ovis, deductum dicere carmen." [17]

There are works of guardedly unambitious proportions and intent that make available even to skeptics the sensibility of total coherence. These are works that gladly embrace the limits of their own finite resources—a fixed vocabulary, an unyielding syntax, a very small number of letters—, self-conscious works that, though circumscribed, are complete, that are in themselves thoroughly designed—in Latin *perfecta*—and they are works that deserve some attention.

Aratus's *Phaenomena* is a poem about the manifestation of design. The casual star-gazer experiences the sky directly and with true insight into what it is, a busy tableau of white specks randomly arranged against a dark background. With instruction and practice he learns to read the heavens, to group stars into the arbitrary patterns of constellations which, once named, are irradicably fixed. For Aratus, though, there is nothing random or arbitrary about the sky. Rather he finds there immanent order in and of Zeus, the god understood doubly as an individual divinity and as Sky itself, that is, as both designer and design. And not order alone but significance:

αὐτὸς γὰρ τά γε σήματ' ἐν οὐρανῷ ἐστήριξεν,
ἄστρα διακρίνας, ἐσκέψατο δ'εἰς ἐνιαυτὸν
ἀστέρας οἵ κε μάλιστα τετυγμένα σημαίνοιεν
ἀνδράσιν ὡράων, ὄφρ'ἔμπεδα πάντα φύωνται. (lines 10–13)

[For it is Zeus who set the signs in the heavens, who demarked constellations and devised for the year the chief stars that give to men the signs of the seasons, so that all things might prosper.]

The constellations are both signs of god's benevolence to be interpreted by men and visible tokens of his coherent design. The signs may be hard to discern or their interpretation obscure, but if the design appears unfinished, it is Aratus's trust that it is complete nonetheless. A passage just before the first acrostic reads

πάντα γὰρ οὔπω
ἐκ Διὸς ἄνθρωποι γινώσκομεν, ἀλλ' ἔτι πολλὰ
κέκρυπται, τῶν αἴ κε θέλῃ καὶ ἐσαυτίκα δώσει
Ζεύς· ὁ γὰρ οὖν γενεὴν ἀνδρῶν ἀναφανδὸν ὀφέλλει,
πάντοθεν εἰδόμενος, πάντη δ' ὅ γε σήματα φαίνων. (768–772)

[We mortals do not yet know all things from Zeus, but much is still hidden which he will grant as he wills; for he aids the race of men openly, manifesting himself on all sides and revealing his signs everywhere.]

As an individual or even a teacher, Aratus remains like other men, the exegete of the heavenly text. But as a didactic poet, he becomes responsible for a text of his own, Zeus-like[18] in his own domain. His resources are a systematizing intelligence and ultimately the

Plexed Artistry: Aratean Acrostics

system of his language. Of this he is well aware; understanding, for example, the ancient link between the recognition of pattern and the first act of language, the process of naming. His description of the work of the primeval astronomer is to the point:

τά τις ἀνδρῶν οὐκέτ' ἐόντων
ἐφράσατ'ἠδ'ἐνόησεν ἅπαντ' ὀνομαστὶ καλέσσαι
ἤλιθα μορφώσας. οὐ γάρ κ'ἐδυνήσατο πάντων
οἰόθι κεκριμένων ὄνομ'εἰπεῖν, οὐδὲ δαῆναι.
πολλοὶ γὰρ πάντῃ, πολέων δ'ἐπὶ ἶσα πέλονται
μέτρα τε καὶ χροιῇ, πάντες γε μὲν ἀμφιέλικτοι.
τῶ καὶ ὁμηγερέας οἱ ἐείσατο ποιήσασθαι
ἀστέρας, ὄφρ'ἐπιτὰξ ἄλλῳ παρακείμενος ἄλλος
εἴδεα σημαίνοιεν. ἄφαρ δ'ὀνομαστὰ γένοντο
ἄστρα, καὶ οὐκέτι νῦν ὑπὸ θαύματι τέλλεται ἀστήρ.
ἀλλ' οἱ μὲν καθαροῖς ἐναρηρότες εἰδώλοισιν
φαίνονται· τὰ δ' ἔνερθε διωκομένοιο Λαγωοῦ
πάντα μάλ'ἠερόεντα καὶ οὐκ ὀνομαστὰ φέρονται. (373–385)

[Someone, long dead, noted the stars and understood to call them all by one name as he grouped them in figures. He could not know all of them singly nor name them, there are so many stars all over, many of the same brightness and color, and all wheel in circles. So he grouped the stars together, so that, set in order, in relation, they might form figures. Thus the constellations got their names, and now no star rises above the horizon, a lone marvel.
The other stars shine grouped in clear figuration, but those beneath the constellation the Hare are all in mist and without names.][19]

A star, isolated and nameless, is obscure and without meaning; significance is born of pattern, and pattern of connection. The last lines of the poem are a warning against the uselessness of an event in isolation:

τῶν μηδὲν κατόνοσσο· καλὸν δ'ἐπὶ σήματι σῆμα
σκέπτεσθαι· μᾶλλον δὲ δυοῖν εἰς ταὐτὸν ἰόντων
ἐλπωρὴ τελέθοι, τριτάτῳ δέ κε θαρσήσειας. . . .
τῶν ἄμυδις πάντων ἐσκεμμένος εἰς ἐνιαυτὸν
οὐδέποτε σχεδίως κεν ἐπ'αἰθέρι τεκμήραιο. (1142–1144, 1153–1154)

[Ignore nothing. It is proper to look for sign confirming sign: when two coincide, that gives you hope; when three, confidence. . . .
Watch all the signs together throughout the year and never will you guess at random.]

The three acrostics of the *Phaenomena* taken together also bear out Aratus's linguistic self-consciousness. Their key words, as I have mentioned, are all crucial terms for his poem and aesthetic—subtlety, totality, and signification; and the acrostics themselves exploit and underscore three basic aspects of the linguistic system he uses—style, grammar, and orthography. But the visual aspect of his language allows him perhaps a greater privilege, to arrange constellations of his own, here black on white but, as bold as Orion or as shy as the hazy Pleiades,[20] still with a clarity analogous to Zeus's.

For Aratus, sight and sense are closely related. The gods can show but their signs must be mediated by speech; they can speak but what they mean must be shown to men. At a critical transition in the poem, the movement earthward from celestial to atmospheric phenomena, Aratus makes this evident by a neat juxtaposition:

πάντη γὰρ τά γε πολλὰ θεοὶ ἄνδρεσσι λέγουσιν.
οὐχ ὁράᾳς; (732–733)

[For on all sides many things do the gods speak to men.
See!]

This theme, its articulation in the *Phaenomena* and in Hellenistic and Roman literature, could be explored at much greater length, but that exploration lies beyond the scope of my intentions.

NOTES

1. A. S. F. Gow, *Bucolici Graeci* (Oxford: Clarendon Press, 1952).

2. "Aratus will live as long as the sun and the moon," *Amores* 1.15.6.

3. There does exist an excellent translation of Aratus into English verse: Stanley Frank Lombardo, *Aratus' Phaenomena: an Introduction and Translation* (Ph.D. diss., University of Texas, 1976). Until this is published, however, the graceless Loeb edition of G. R. Mair (London: W. Heinemann, 1921) is the most easily available to the Greekless reader. All translations in this article are my own.

4. The "Besantinou Bomos" of Roman date, Gow, *Bucolici Graeci*, p. 184. While acrostic poems are not rare in Greek literature, Latin authors seem to have taken to them with more enthusiasm; from the hoary father of Latin literature Ennius, whose acrostic signature—Quintus Ennius fecit—Cicero records (*de Div.* 2.111), through a contemporary of Constantine, Publilius Optatianus Porfyrius, who bore prodigies: see, for example, his eighteenth poem.

For Vergil's recreation of one Aratean acrostic, see *Georgics* 1.429–433, and E. L. Brown, *Numeri Vergiliani, Collection Latomus* 63 (1963): 102–4.

5. "Sur un Acrostiche d'Aratos," *Revue des Etudes Anciennes* 62 (1960): 48–61.

6. Jacques's remarks on the programmatic content of this whole passage are excellent. See also the valuable comments of E. D. Francis, "Aratos ʺΑΓΡΥΝΟΣ

Plexed Artistry: Aratean Acrostics

```
ALMETVASLAVRVSAETASSVSTOLLETINASTRA
LVCETVASIGNESFASTVSSINELIMITECONSVL
MARTESERENVSHABESREIECTOMVNIAGRAIVM
ETMEDIPRAESTASINCENSVMSCEPTRAREDIRE
TORVAGETASCAMPOCLARVSVTLVMINAPERDIT
VVLTCVRVOTVRMAEFELIXSVACOMMINVSICTV
ARMENIIDVXFERRELEVISSOLTEQVOQVEPILA
SICETVICTAREFERTEXORTOSDACIAFRANCOS
LEGETVVSTONSORHENVSTIBIGERMINATEXVL
AGMINATFLORVMSVBEANTQVIMVRMVREBELLA
VINCEREFLORENTILATIALESSARMATADVCTV
REXTIBIPOSSEGETASVISODATLIMITEVLTOR
VIDITTESVMMVMCOLVMENQVAVELIFERAESTV
SERVSINOCEANIPRESSITIVGANYSIAPONTVS
ATQVERVDISRADIISCITLVXEXORTATROPAEA
ENGAVDENTPIETATEALTISPARSPERPETEAGE
TVVATEMFIRMESDICTVSTENVNCLYRACANTET
AVCTADEOVIRTVSMVSASMAGISORNATAPERTA
SOLVMVOTANOTISLATESVAROMVLADATPLEBS
SANCTATVISCLIOPERMISCETVOTATROPAEIS
VISITVRETCRESCITPICTORVMGRATIACANTV
SITVISVICINISPERTHYLENGRATIAPOLLENS
TALISFIXASVISSIGNISLYRAMVNERAGESTAT
ORSAPARIVATESQVAEPERFERTDELIERYTHMO
LVMINEMVRICEOVENERANDVSDVXERITVTSOL
LEGIBVSVTIANITENEASAVVSORBETRIBVNAL
EGREGIOSTITVLOSPIETATISHABEBISAMORE
TOTFRETAPACISAPEXMVTARIMVNEREGAVDET
INDIACLAVIGERILATIVMVVLTTANGERENAVI
NILEVSMESSORSVATRADITCASTRAVELAGMEN
ARCTOSQVAMCARPINOSCETVIXHAEMVSINORA
SICISTISCVLTVSINREMCVRVANTIBVSENSES
TENIVEAIVVATARCEFRVIPONTIDECVSAVGET
ROMASORORVETERESTVSCOSQVOSORETVEMVR
ALMETVASLAVRVSAETASSVSTOLLETINASTRA
```

and Vergil (*Georg.* 1,424–437)," forthcoming in *Hermes*. I am grateful to Prof. Francis for permission to read and cite this paper.

7. "Nicander's Signature," *Classical Quarterly* 22 (1928): 114.

8. W. C. Helmbold, *American Journal of Philology* 76 (1955): 110. Helmbold's conjecture was frankly made to avoid a defective acrostic; he confessed himself unable, however, to remedy the difficulty in the fourth line. J.-M. Jacques, in "Les 'Alexipharmaques' de Nicandre," *Revue des Etudes Anciennes* 57 (1955): 20, conjectures ναὶ μήν for σὺν δὲ καὶ, and ἀσκηροῦ for καστηνοῦ: if he is correct, the acrostic is complete. A. S. F. Gow and A. F. Scholfield, *Nicander: The Poems and Poetical Fragments* (Cambridge: At the University Press, 1953) print the initial letters as read by Lobel.

Perhaps understanding is needed rather than correction.

9. Brown, *Numeri Vergiliani*, p. 109.

10. Ibid., p. 102–14.

11. The literature on literary games is now of great volume and disheartening sophistication. A reader might begin with the lucid first chapter of Elizabeth Sewell, *The Field of Nonsense* (London: Chatto and Windus, 1952); or, in a different vein, with *Game, Play, Literature*, Yale French Studies 41 (1969); or, best of all, with Francis Huxley, *The Raven and the Writing Desk* (London: Thames and Hudson, 1976).

12. V. Nabokov, *Pale Fire* (New York: Putnam, 1962), p. 62–63.

13. See Paul Fournel, *Clefs pour la littérature potentielle* (Paris: Editions Denöel, 1972); Oulipo, *La littérature potentielle: Créations re-créations récréations* (Paris: Gallimard, 1973); Harry Mathews, "Oulipo," *Word Ways* 9 (May 1976): 67–74; Martin Gardner, "Mathematical Games," *Scientific American* 236 (February 1977): 121–26.

14. By Georges Perec, in *La littérature potentielle*, p. 101–6.

15. *Cent mille milliards de poèmes* (Paris: Gallimard, 1961).

16. An example concocted by Martin Gardner, "Mathematical Games," p. 123: the first sentences of *Moby Dick* transformed according to the Noun-plus-7 algorithm as it's called—

> Call me islander. Some yeggs ago—never mind how long precisely—having little or no Mongol in my purulence, and nothing particular to interest me on shortbread, I thought I would sail about a little and see the watery partiality of the worriment.

Or the first noun/last noun exchange using Melville's first chapter—

> Call me air. Some hills ago—never mind how long precisely—having little or no phantoms in my whale, and nothing particular to interest me on processions, I thought I would sail about a little and see the watery soul of the purpose.

Beautiful, whatever it is.

17. "When I was singing of kings and battles, Apollo plucked my ear and said, 'A shepherd, Tityrus, should let his sheep grow fat but keep his poems slender.'" Vergil, *Eclogues* 6.3–5; a translation of the advice given Callimachus (*Aetia* 1.23–24):

$$\mathring{α}οιδέ, τὸ μὲν θύος ὅττι πάχιστον$$
$$θρέψαι, τὴν Μοῦσαν δ'ὠγαθὲ λεπταλέην.$$

in which *deductum* represents λεπταλέην, a version of λεπτή.

18. This equation may be suggested early in the poem:

$$\text{'Ἐκ Διὸς ἀρχώμεσθα, τὸν οὐδεποτ'ἄνδρες ἐῶμεν}$$
$$\text{ἄρρητον} \qquad \text{(ll. 1-2)}$$

If APPHTON conceals APATON, then the true author of pattern is indeed "not unnamed."

19. John Hollander has cited this passage as a note to his poem "The Great Bear." See *Spectral Emanations: New and Selected Poems* (New York: Atheneum, 1978), pp. 237–38. It is not surprising that Hollander, the foremost living practitioner of the figurative poem (among other distinctions), should have recognized Aratus.

20. Aratus's description of this group (ll. 254–267) as an incomplete constellation one of whose stars is missing provides a neat analogue to the third acrostic.

FOUR

A "RAFT OF TROUBLE": WORD AND DEED IN *HUCKLEBERRY FINN*
Laurence B. Holland

CRITICISM of *Huckleberry Finn* has defined a consensus that the book's closing section is seriously flawed, for even those who find the last twelve chapters to be coherent in conception agree that the incidents relating Tom's "evasion" scheme for rescuing Jim are indulgently overwritten and in execution are as embarrassing as Hemingway claimed they were in *The Green Hills of Africa.* After Chapter 31, he declared, "the rest is just cheating," and he advised people to stop reading the book at the point, apparently at the end of Chapter 31, where "Jim is stolen from the boys" and sold by the fraudulent King.[1] The chapters are nevertheless well enough executed to bear rereading, and the scenes that terminate Tom's evasion scheme are so well done and so vivid that they demand more attention than Hemingway's injunction tempts us to give. In themselves they provide a significant context for the disclosure that Miss Watson has freed Jim in her will, and they illuminate the connections between the final section and earlier parts of the book and the profound folly on which Twain's novel rests. Moreover, the incidents help reveal how Twain's idiom and narrative form create the moving if somberly comic and ironic vision that lies at the heart of Twain's masterpiece.

What *Huckleberry Finn* is about is the process, with its attendant absurdities, of setting a free man free. This is the issue from the moment Huck, born free but staging and feigning his own death, seeks refuge on Jackson's Island, though the book seldom speaks explicitly about this matter in terms such as "freedom" and "liberation." It speaks more often instead of "rescuing" and "saving" important characters. The theme is figured chiefly, however, in the central case of Jim, without being confined exclusively to him, and it is first phrased definitively in the closing section (in Chapter 42), when Jim's legal emancipation is divulged: "Tom Sawyer had gone to all that trouble and bother to set a free nigger free!" The process of setting a free man free is left unfinished at the end, but the closing section does not wrench the book from its course; it reveals in sharper light the profound irony that governs the book and which we should avoid simplifying. The central importance of this irony to the coherence of the book is obscured, I think, by a genetic approach to Twain's narrative even in such incisive analyses as those of Henry Nash Smith and Leo Marx, which emphasize Huck's vernacular speech, Huck's role as narrator, and Twain's difficulties in finishing his manuscript, to the comparative neglect of Jim's role and the scapegoating that is entailed by Twain's comic strategies.[2] The irony is shaped by Twain's desperately felt need for liberation and by a mixture of scorn for, and acquiescence in, the impulses, habits, and institutions that leave the quest for freedom still unsatisfied and all but paralyzed. The irony is deepened by Twain's tacit acknowledgment of his own, Huck's, and Jim's involvement with Tom Sawyer's world, and by Twain's recognition of the moral implications of his stance toward his subject and of the fictive form that generates his vision.

At the risk of reading the book backward, let us begin with the incidents in Chapter 40, which tells of Huck's and Jim's decision to risk Jim's exposure in order to seek a doctor for Tom. Tom's fantastic escape plans (inspired by the tales and historical accounts he takes for models) have called for enemies, and his insane "nonnamous letter," warning the Phelpses of the impending escape, has brought to the cabin a posse of fifteen farmers equipped with dogs and armed with guns. They shoot at the fleeing threesome and wound Tom in the leg before the three can make it to safety on the raft. Before the fact of Tom's wound is divulged, Jim is allowed to lavish praise on the beauty of the plan and its execution, and Huck is allowed a sigh of relief at precisely the moment when he steps onto the raft and proclaims his joy at Jim's liberation. But in view of the frequency with which Jim has had to be rescued before (to say nothing of what is shortly forthcoming), Huck's exclamation is as comic as it is genuine: "*Now*, old Jim, you're free *again*, and I bet you won't ever be a slave no more." It is somberly comic not only because it is overconfident but also because the recurring necessity of freeing Jim, underscored by Twain's italics of *"now"* and *"again,"* has become by this time at once a moral imperative and an ineffectual routine. Both that moral pressure and that sense of futility lie deep within *Huckleberry Finn*.

The incident continues as Tom's excitement mounts, doubled by his discovery that he has been shot and leading him to disregard his wound in surrender to his fancies. With the cockiness of a young executive and the lunacy of Tom-foolishness he is still superintending the affair at the end of the chapter. His comparison of Jim's rescue to that of King Louis XVI, however, embedded though it is in Tom's indulgent fantasies, has ominous implications. It is disturbing because Jim's royal French counterpart was not saved from the guillotine and also because Tom's first aid—he is bandaging himself with a shirt left behind by the Duke—recalls the fraudulent King and Duke who in Chapter 19 called out from shore, begged Huck to "save their lives," and instantly were rescued from the "trouble" on shore and admitted to the raft.

The insecurity of the raft as a refuge for Huck and Jim, and the inseparable mixture of comic antics (foolish in both word and deed) with desperately urgent matters, are of central importance throughout *Huckleberry Finn*. In this late incident Tom's foolishness is significantly related to the matching folly of Huck and Jim, who decide, despite Tom's strenuous objections and attempts to block their efforts, that Huck should venture to shore to bring a doctor to Tom. Saving Tom, freeing him from danger, is taking precedence over setting Jim free. This decision—the deed that results in Jim's capture and shortly threatens him first with hanging and then with being sold at auction—is one of the most important events in the book and it is made by Huck and Jim in a moment of deliberation that Twain renders in telling details. These details underscore the fact that the decision is mutual and that Jim is given the crucial task of putting it into words.

After "consulting—and thinking" together for a solemn moment in silence, Huck is certain what Jim will say but insists: "Say it, Jim." And Jim, revealing to Huck that he is admirably "white inside," reveals their mutual folly, speaking without a trace of pretense or hollowness in the dialect that Twain renders so painstakingly. Taking Tom as a model of unselfish conduct, Jim asks whether Tom, were he the runaway slave, would urge friends to "save me" instead of helping a wounded comrade. Jim concludes that role-model Tom would not say that and then concludes: "Well, den, is *Jim* gwyne to say it? No, sah—I doan' budge a step out'n dis place, 'dout a *doctor*; not if it's forty year!"

Even before the reader learns (or remembers) that their decision has dire consequences for Jim, their folly is transparent in taking Tom as a model of selflessness, since Tom's antics consistently assign to himself the role of heroic superintendent of his adventures. Yet his wound is a fact and in the days before penicillin it is serious; the Doctor later wants medical assistance but does not dare abandon Tom to get it. What makes Tom ludicrous in this scene—his willingness to disregard his own danger—also lends some support to Jim's feeling that Tom would not put his own safety ahead of a friend's, but does not justify the full measure of heroism that Jim and Huck credit to him. Both the folly of Huck's and Jim's decision and its moral rightness are sanctioned by the episode, which nowhere suggests that Huck and Jim should follow Tom's fantasy-ridden advice by neglecting his wound and continuing their flight. And in reaching this decision Huck and Jim are as close in rapport as they have ever been. The bond between them has been close before—when promising not to disclose each other's whereabouts, when relaxing on the raft, when Huck humbles himself before Jim or listens to that black King Lear's penitent confession of cruelty to a daughter whose mute silence he misunderstood. The bond between them is close again when Jim hugs Huck in joy after their separation, and when they decide finally to cut loose from the King and Duke. But now they actually make a deliberate decision in utter reciprocity and do so in words that Huck asks Jim to speak.

The serious consequences of their decision come to light in Chapter 42 when the Doctor returns with Tom feverish on a stretcher and with Jim tied and guarded by the posse of men who recaptured him on the raft. Twain's denouement, the disclosure that Miss Watson legally freed Jim two months earlier, casts the entire narrative in a sharper light, and certain details in which he describes the capture of Jim serve as echoes both of Tom's evasion and of the trip down the river—an earlier "evasion" as it is now made to appear—on the raft.

Before divulging the fact that Jim is already legally free, Twain does nothing to relax the danger that Jim faces. Though in peril frequently before, Jim is now threatened with hanging by some of the posse who wish to make him an object lesson to other Negroes. Moreover, they blame Jim alone for the "raft of trouble," as Huck calls it, which has overwhelmed the Phelpses and the neighborhood, in their ignorance making Jim the scapegoat for the project which Tom, with Huck's grudging assistance, has launched. Jim is saved only by the reasoning that Twain was to treat in its full nightmarish absurdity at the end of *Pudd'nhead Wilson*: Jim's legal owners would demand payment if their property were destroyed by hanging; therefore Jim must be spared and held for a proper period of time before being sold, if unclaimed, at auction. Huck is at once pained and helpless in recounting Jim's reimprisonment. The cruelty is condemned implicitly, and challenged by Huck's intention to tell Aunt Sally about Jim's service to Tom, but it is not challenged in act. One of Huck's longest sentences in the book renders at once the cruelties inflicted on Jim (the cursing and cuffing) and also Huck's anguished paralysis at witnessing Jim's confinement, which seems ominously unbreachable and final. And his account persistently recalls Jim's treatment earlier in the cabin by the Phelpses and by Tom and Huck, making clear that Jim's treatment now, though far worse, is precisely similar to what it was then. This time he is tied with heavier chains to the cabin itself instead of to the bedstead, he is now given only bread and water to eat, the escape hole is filled up, and now a bulldog and armed white guards, instead of approachable Negroes, are posted. But he is put in the "same" cabin; he is chained "again."

What Huck's long and apprehensive sentence prepares for is the Doctor's recollection of his discovery of Jim aboard the raft—a "yarn," as Huck calls it, that is intended to arouse admiration and kinder treatment for Jim, but whose effect on the posse is minimal; it persuades them merely to stop cussing Jim. Huck's highest hope is merely that they would add meat and greens to Jim's diet, and lighten the load of chains, and even this proves sanguine. Huck thinks it best not to "mix in," though he hopes that when he tells the Doctor's "yarn" to Aunt Sally it will move her to make Jim more comfortable.

One reason why the Doctor's account is significant is that it is one of the most moving and genuine tributes to Jim in the book, and one of the most vivid glimpses of Jim's service to a friend while "resking his freedom to do it." Rendered in colloquial speech as authentic as Huck's, it functions to strengthen the reader's admiration of Jim's heroism. A second reason, however, is that the Doctor's sympathy is wholly contained within the confines of loyalty to the slavery system. His statement returns at the end to the reductive and negative statement with which he opens his recollection: "He an't no bad nigger, gentlemen; that's what I think about him." Yet it includes a strangely tender, nakedly simple description of Jim's betrayal. The glimpse of Jim's betrayal that the Doctor gives serves more vividly than the news of his sale by the King to reveal and condemn implicitly the earlier betrayals which have occurred in the course of the book. When some men unexpectedly row by the raft at dawn, Jim "as good luck would have it" is sitting beside Tom in a familiar posture "with his head propped on his knees, sound asleep," and the Doctor recalls that "I motioned them in, quiet, and they slipped up on him and tied him before he knew what he was about, and we never had no trouble."

The facts that the Doctor's tribute to Jim is notably *ex post facto*, and that the events of the summer have culminated in Jim's recapture, reinforce the irony of Twain's masterpiece. The raft that is now vulnerable to incursions by the Doctor and the posse has before been vulnerable to the King and the Duke, who along with Jim and Huck turn the raft into an image of the civilization with its discontents on shore. Efforts to protect Jim have had to be repeated repeatedly before. Indeed Huck's dream of freedom—escape from civilization, liberation from the burdensome six thousand dollars which was the reward he had won in *Tom Sawyer*, and escape from Pap and surrogate or adoptive parents—is countered by another dream of freedom projected in Jim: his longing to escape from slavery and enter *into* the civilization that chafes Huck, Jim's clinging to the sacred five-cent piece he wears around his neck and his desire *for* the money, the eight hundred dollars, that would buy freedom for his family, Jim's longing to be reunited with his wife and daughter and to *assume* the role of husband and father. These antithetical dreams of freedom are sustained in an uneasy ambiance through to the end of the novel.

In this context, Tom's evasion scheme, in its very extremes of indulgent excess, are appropriate indeed. Tom's antics confer the burden of heroism on Jim but make a cruel and diseased mockery of it. Jim's is the burden of Orpheus to charm (with a "jews-harp") the rats and serpents that flock around him, but in Tom's fantasies Jim winds up with the head of a rattlesnake in his mouth. Tom's antics are in effect the rehearsal for the ominous enslavement that ensues when Jim is enchained "again" in the "same" cabin. Jim's enslavement, and the process of liberation offered in the book—Jim in chains in the cabin, Jim disguised as King Lear or a sick Arab aboard the raft, Jim chained on the raft pretending to be a recaptured runaway—both make a scapegoat of Jim and are virtual mirror images of each other. Liberation dissolves into enslavement and they come close, without actually doing so, to cancelling each other out. Jim stands at the end, legally free but without the substance of freedom envisioned for him by William Blake in "America: A Prophecy": "Let the enchained soul, shut up in darkness and in sighing . . ./Rise and look out; his chains are loose, his dungeon doors are open;/And let his wife and children return from the oppressor's scourge." Jim stands free but severed from his wife and daughter, all but forgotten by Huck, with nothing like Lear's one hundred knights or Orpheus's lyre, with little but the forty bucks given him by Tom to insure the promise of William Blake and others who have helped invent the American dream. The tortured irony that defines Jim's predicament encompasses also Huck, who at the end stands immobile, the possessor still as Jim informs him of his six grand, fantasizing about an escape to the Territory which seems increasingly impossible of attainment. Huck would go to "the territory ahead of the rest." But that Territory is not a green continent accessible in space but a fleeting moment receding into a past now "Forty or Fifty Years Ago." By the time Huck got there, "the rest"—the Kings and Dukes, the Tom Sawyers, probably the Aunt Sallies—would soon be there in numbers to hail him and seek accommodation on the raft.

In such a world of balked hopes and tortured expectations, Miss Watson's deathbed decision to free Jim is singularly fitting. Even the suddenness, indeed the sportiveness, of its introduction in the text is appropriate to the pre–Civil War era when such emancipations were often afterthoughts, so to speak, all too infrequent, always tardy, and no doubt, like the Emancipation of 1862, prompted in part by mixed motives. There is nothing careless, nor self-indulgent, about Twain's treatment of the incident in Chapter 42. Good-natured Tom, returning to consciousness and (all hope) sanity, divulges the information instantly when he hears that Jim is in danger of being sold: Miss Watson was "ashamed" of her intent to sell Jim and "said so"; just before she died she "set him free in her will." However questionable her motives (they are usually questioned, though there is little evidence about them), these details are telling in a narration where declaring things in spoken speech, willed intentions, and the activity of writing are crucial matters, as they have become long before "yours truly," Huck Finn, stops the story that has become his epistle to the world for the simple reason that "there is nothing more to write about." The reality Huck summons up in the book includes the prose styles and other styles to which Huck, and "The Author" of the opening notice about dialects used in the book, so often draw attention: Pap's way of speaking, Tom's style of behavior which Huck usually admires, fashions in poetry and painting at the Grangerfords' house, the "ignorantest kind of words and pictures," charcoal graffiti, in the room where Pap's corpse is recognized by Jim in Chapter 9. It includes the Doctor's "yarn," as Huck calls it, and the countless tales Huck tells during his trip down the river, to say nothing of the crucial incident to which I have already attached importance when Jim's saying, and the silent decision jointly made with Huck that it articulates, define at once Jim's moral heroism and his folly. The virtu if not the virtue of Tom's evasion scheme is, as Huck grudgingly says in Chapter 34, that it will "make . . . talk," and making *talk*, or the illusion of it as Professor Richard Bridgman cautions us to say,[3] is important to Huck's and Twain's colloquial idiom.

More importantly the narrative proper opens with a bibliographical ploy that locates Huck as the figure in a book named *Tom Sawyer*, and in Chapter 31 Huck's dramatic decisions—to turn Jim over to the authorities, then to tear up the letter in which he had articulated that first decision and to give over reforming—these decisions are made in a counterpoint of written and spoken speech. Whether genuine and durable or not, Huck's moral commitments are made not in severance from his civilization but in an entanglement, more properly an engagement, with its very foundation, namely language. He makes his first decision in an experiment with written language, then undoes it in an action which redeems, for brief moments, the Widow Douglas's injunction in Chapter 3 to "help other people, and do everything I could for other people, and look out for them all the time, and never think about myself." His famous declaration about going to hell, presumably spoken but like everything in the book inscribed in the print that issued from type fonts and presses, is made in the only moral vocabulary Huck has, which folds both the Sunday School or Revival Sermon vocabulary, and Huck's colloquial idiom, into the phrase "go to hell."

This conjunction of spoken speech, decision-making, and writing relates to Miss Watson's will in ways I shall return to presently. But another strikingly controlled notation about Miss Watson's deed—namely, that she did this "two months ago"—illuminates a peculiar resiliency in the prose style of *Huckleberry Finn* and intricacies in the temporal dimension of the narration that I should dwell on briefly. As for the matter of style, what I wish to insist on is that the ostensible "now" of the present tense in the book, and the ostensible "then" of the past tenses, enforce each other insofar as they can be distinguished in the prose, but that they virtually dissolve into each other without actually doing so, and that what Huck presents to us, perhaps obviously, is an act of memory which is sometimes identified explicitly as such in the phrasing.

The stance of *Huckleberry Finn* is that of direct address, careful and conscious, to both the subject and the reader. It places Huck in a continuous present, as we usually call it, before the reader. He talks to us at the opening, telling us in the "here and now" to look him up in the index to *Tom Sawyer*, and addresses us at the end, talking to us about what Tom is doing now and what he plans to do now, signing off as "yours truly" (his narration impulsively becomes epistolary) even after noting "the end." But Huck at times tells us that he is remembering things in a style that sustains the illusion of the "there and then": "I can't ever get it out of my memory, the sight of them poor miserable girls and niggers" (Chapter 27). The very illusion of remembering is rendered by the style, even when nothing is said explicitly about remembering. The rightfully famous description of Huck's father, Pap, in Chapter 5 is not a sudden response, not the "first jolt" or shock in the so-called immediate present of Pap's ominous return, but a deliberate recapitulation, mounting in intensity, of Pap's appearance, composed on the basis of frequent confrontations and thoroughly digested, considered details: "He was most fifty, and he looked it. His hair was long and tangled and greasy, and hung down, and you could see his eyes shining through like he was behind vines. It was all black, no gray; so was his long, mixed-up whiskers. There warn't no color in his face, where his face showed; it was white; not like another man's white, but a white to make a body sick, a white to make a body's flesh crawl—a tree-toad white, a fish-belly white."

Huck's remembering includes repressed memories of things he refuses to enlarge upon and anticipations of the future: "It made me so sick I nearly fell out of the tree. I ain't agoing to tell all that happened—it would make me sick again, if I was to do that. I wished I hadn't ever come ashore that night to see such things. I ain't ever going to get shut of them—lots of times I dream about them" (Chapter 18). Often the vividness of the present inheres in the act of telling or talking to us whereas the incidents spoken of take place in the past: "the way I lit out and shinned for the road in the dark there ain't nobody can tell"—there ain't nobody can tell 'now' about the way he lit out back 'then.' To combine the effect of the vivid present and the remembered past Twain often uses one of the easiest displacements known in colloquial speech: "Well, when they was all gone the King he asks. . . ." (Chapter 26) in which past and present tenses are interchangeable. In the famous and beautiful passage at the opening of Chapter 19, where Huck in orderly fashion describes the combination of pleasure and apprehensiveness in life aboard the raft, what Huck "could" hypothetically see, what he "would" recurrently see each day, what he "maybe" detected in the sign-language of the river's surfaces, and what he does sense apprehensively as threats to his safety on this far from idyllic raft—these modes and tenses dissolve into each other: "We would watch the lonesomeness of the river, and kind of lazy along, and by-and-by lazy off to sleep. Wake up, by-and-by, and look to see what done it, and maybe see a steamboat, coughing along upstream. . . ." A few paragraphs later, just after invoking a sky "speckled with stars" and the darkness brightened by a "world of sparks" from a steamboat's chimneys: "Just as I was passing a place where a kind of cow-path crossed the crick, here comes a couple of men tearing up the path as tight as they could foot it." The King and Duke are about to ask for and be offered instant refuge on the raft.

The resilience of this style, which makes possible a vivid presentness in narration fuelling a process of remembering, and which translates imperceptibly the counterpoint of telling and listening in a fictive present into shared recognition and reenactment of Huck's remembered past, heightens the significance of a feature we too often neglect in considering Twain's masterpiece, namely that it is an historical novel which early draws attention to that fact. Huck's insistence that we refer for his provenance to the earlier book *Tom Sawyer* is in keeping with the cast back into the past which is launched on the title page: "Scene: The Mississippi Valley. Time: Forty to Fifty Years Ago." The future imperatives in the "Notice" to the reader posted by Twain's delegate the "Chief of Ordinance" ("persons attempting to find a plot in it will be shot"), and the note "Explanatory" about its dialects in the present tense signed by "The Author," are already governed by this extension of temporal perspective to encompass the movement back from 1885 to the decade straddling 1840. Whether or not Twain was indulging in the nostalgia that the novelist Wright Morris has found a threat to all American fiction,[4] in *Huckleberry Finn* the past of, say, 1840 stands in a troubled, strained relation with the writing of the book or its publication in 1885. "Forty to Fifty Years Ago" in effect defines a dilemma which is dramatized, in the narration, by the quite exact, seemingly gratuitous specification that Miss Watson's declaration of repentance and her liberation of Jim in her will took place "two months" ago. This fact does not belatedly skew the written structure of the book but buttresses the principles that constitute it. It brings 1885, in its relation to 1840, to the verge of discontinuity but sustains a perilous continuum in which "now" and "then," "now" and "again," both challenge and engage each other.[5]

Once Twain can be presumed to have stumbled or decided upon this feature of his denouement, he did not arrange a recent demise for Miss Watson, though her dying as recently as four or five weeks before the concluding episode would have provided Tom with the safety of legality he enjoys when perpetrating his evasion scheme, while making her death virtually simultaneous with Huck's tearing up his letter to her, his decision not to inform on Jim. Instead, Twain's timing of her death assigns a priority in time to her words and deeds, her spoken declaration and her written will, which haunt the resolution of the novel, stir and agitate its rhythms. The priority of Miss Watson's will underscores the fact that Huck's bold and solemn decision was not to free Jim, in any tangible and full sense, but vaguely to protect him, that it was not as crucial as Huck had thought at the time or not crucial in ways he thought, that his decision was not as dangerous and courageous as it has seemed. Miss Watson's will gives the status of a ritual gesture to Huck's momentous decision, places at a distance the drama and urgency of Jim's legal fate, relegates to the past any opportunity to give Jim the freedom he deserves. Insofar as Miss Watson's written will is moved further back from the closing episodes of Twain's denouement, it is removed too from the years in the 1870s and 1880s when Twain, who never freed a slave in his life, was ensconced in Hartford writing *Huckleberry Finn*. By seeming sportive and unexpected, and distant, Miss Watson's act enforces the sense of futility that deepens toward the end of *Huckleberry Finn*. The option to write out or inscribe Jim's legal freedom was Miss Watson's in 1840. Moreover the chance of setting a freed Negro free seems dim in Chapters 42 and 43, with Jim in chains again, then freed suddenly to stand jobless and alone, with nothing but a meal, Tom's forty-dollar payment, and the prospect of a camping trip in the Territory with the boys to satisfy his dream of freedom in a promised land. Yet the task of redeeming Jim's legal freedom, fulfilling the promise that legal freedom makes possible, that unfinished business haunts and troubles the denouement of Twain's novel. The sequence of incidents that have come so near to nought in 1840 and stand so far back in time from 1885 in the temporal perspective of the book bring this historical fiction to the brink of irrelevance for the post–Civil War world. Yet precisely because it verges on irrelevance it speaks with all the more pointed relevance across the span of forty or fifty years in 1885 to define the task and impose the charge of setting a nation of freedmen free. The flukish fact of Jim's legal freedom, and the failure of his world to flesh it out with the family, the opportunities, and the community which would give it meaning, define with haunting and painful relevance, and with absurd precision, the problem of setting a free Negro free, which is the pressing problem, in all its extensions, in post–Civil War America and more recent decades.

In forging this timeliness from the receding past, accommodating the tensions between Tom's sportive fantasies and the somber realities they mirror in American society, or accomodating the tensions between the diverging dreams of freedom that are suspended in the comradeship of Jim and Huck, *Huckleberry Finn* becomes not so much a novel as a romance. In saying that I resort to a binary terminology I do not like, and particularly I would not want to imply that the book is any less novelistic in its textures and strategies for being a romance. What I have in mind are basic features of imaginative fiction that Henry James insisted were possible in either the so-called novel or the so-called romance but which are usually denominated by the latter term: the evocation of the "possible" and visionary rather than the "actual"; fiction's status as fiction: its daring, as Hawthorne defined the task of the romancer, to locate itself "on the utmost verge of a precipitous absurdity."[6] *Huckleberry Finn* generates and yields a vision, a possibility made real in language though not yet actualized in the behavior of Huck and Tom or Mark Twain on Asylum Hill in Hartford, nor in the relations generally of white, black, or brown people since. It creates a vision which would redeem the promise of Jim's legal freedom, would redeem the failed and failing effort to set a free Negro free, and it sanctions the promise of that vision, makes it the moral imperative, the willed inscription, that governs this fiction. It does this by pushing all the fictive conventions it uses, including what we usually recognize as novelistic ones, to the limit where they become a fully imaginative act. The very plausibility of its illusionistic representation—the fullness with which this plausibility is achieved in the river landscapes, the spruced-up domestic interiors or the dingy rooms aboard floating abandoned houses, the untidy yards of marginal farms, and above all the colloquial idiom of Huck and the other characters as well—the fully representational illusion that this book prints to us is a kind of fictive magic, a lie, which yields *The Adventures of Huckleberry Finn* and the vision burgeoning within it. It is all the more magical for seeming not to be, for seeming to concede priority to a reality independent of the imagination. And the text is haunted by the recognition of its status as fiction and of the moral hazards entailed in the enterprise of fiction. Indeed it is haunted by the implications of the particular narrative structure that Twain devised for his masterpiece.

Twain begins to play with the matter of lying fantasy on the first page when Huck wryly alludes to the intrusion of lies, or more cautiously "stretchers," in *The Adventures of Tom Sawyer*. Even earlier, faking it in the guise of a deputy "Chief of Ordinance," Twain has taken the preposterous stance of one who will banish and shoot misguided readers, the stance taken in Chapter Two by fancy-ridden Tom Sawyer who declares that intruders on his gang "must be sued" and second-offenders "must be killed." One paradigm for Twain's narration in the book is the episode where Huck and Jim make a decision in silence while Huck delegates to Jim the task of speaking it in words, and then Jim for them both engages in a flight of fancy that is an act at once of folly and of heroism, imagining for Tom a freedom from self that exceeds the facts. Twain, like Huck in this instance, remains ostensibly and actually silent throughout the narration—"Say it, Huck"—creating the lie that Huck speaks or writes the book which unfolds, word by printed word, in the silence of fiction before us.

Twain's narration, and the complicity in the world he projects that is revealed in his narrative form, are illuminated by a hilarious and profoundly revealing essay he wrote in 1882, "The Decay in the Art of Lying." There, addressing Hartford historians whom he said were masters of the art, he defined the lie as a "Virtue . . . , the fourth Grace, the Tenth Muse," and, declaring with guilty abandon that lying is an unavoidable "necessity of our circumstances," he called on all to "train ourselves to lie thoughtfully . . . , to lie for others' advantage, and not our own; to lie gracefully and graciously, not . . . clumsily . . . ," to lie not "with pusillanimous mien" but "firmly" without "being ashamed of our high calling." He defined one particular category of lie that has a particular bearing on *Huckleberry Finn*: the "silent lie," the "deception which one conveys by keeping still and concealing the truth," or what he called in another essay ("My First Lie and How I Got Out of It") the "lie of silent assertion."[7]

On such a "lie of silent assertion" depends the closing section of Twain's book which so disturbs us, when Tom Sawyer starts to blurt out the fact of Jim's emancipation but then smothers it in silence.[8] By his "lie of silent assertion" Tom is able to stage the rescue of Jim which is so cruel and intended to be so entertaining: the "evasion" with its pretentions to righteousness, its tawdry melodrama, which produces the "raft of trouble" at the end; the fakery and sport which debase Jim and then endanger Jim and Tom both; the "fun" which "makes talk" and which Huck, disguised as Tom, helps perpetrate; the folly which Twain exposes to the shame of our condemnation. Tom-foolishness indeed. Aunt Sally as well as Huck detects the absurdity of "setting a free nigger free." Twain could hardly have overlooked the fact that his own *Adventures* and their suspense are founded on the same silent lie. However much his art depended on improvisation, his improvisations were those of an expert performer who by the 1880s could anticipate the dubieties of fiction and the risks of his own methods. When revising his narrative and giving it the endorsement of his pseudonymn, he knew the final shape it had taken. Miss Watson, around 1840, had legally freed Jim but neither Tom nor Twain had told readers so until the last minute.

Moreover it was Twain who stopped Tom in mid-sentence—"Say it, Tom"—and Twain it was, though with more complex motives than Tom's, who thought up the crude sport that is condemned in Tom, the "adventure" as Tom calls it to which Twain devoted so much of *The Adventures of Huckleberry Finn*. Twain's conscience is therefore stirred not only by the guilt he feels as a Tom Sawyerish, fish-belly white citizen who never freed a slave in his life, but by the lie he perpetrated in the very act of forming his fiction, holding to the logic of its suspense, founding its entertainment and its moral drama on Tom's crude sport and his "lie of silent assertion." As it approaches its completion, the fiction becomes fully confessional. *Mea culpa* (1840): Miss Watson's writing, not Tom Sawyer, not Mark Twain, freed the Negro Jim.

Huck Finn likewise, when he looks back and remembers the incident on the raft when he tore up the letter to Miss Watson, now knows that Jim has already been freed. But to reenact the drama which constitutes his heroism, to recreate it in its vividness and moral urgency, Huck must in memory keep to the lie of silence. The very elemental form of the narration inescapably involves its narrator and its author in a fraud or lie and can be made a worthy or redeeming act only if the lie generates in language a vision, with its moral pressure, which extends beyond the facts of incident and warm companionship which the language presents. And the lie can be made to have that effect because the silence is not only a deception but an expressive form which yields concerns, recognitions, and aspirations beyond anything made explicit. The same willed silence which enables Tom and Twain to hide facts is an enabling form. The result is that the thirty-first chapter, rendering Huck's crucial decisions, burgeons with a pressure of moral urgency and commitment which most of us have felt but which exceeds anything actually true of Huck's behavior before or since. The actuality of Huck's feelings and behavior since leaving the river, as occasionally on it, have fallen short of the vision presented in this chapter. Indeed the very chapter dramatizes also Huck's lapse into passivity, vague protestations and improvisations, and neglect of Jim that are so conspicuous later. All Huck literally does is to perform an essentially negative act, deciding not to disclose Jim's whereabouts. One of the most terrifying moments in the book, appearing directly after Huck tears up his letter to Miss Watson, occurs when Huck's grief-stricken tribute to Jim takes the form of claiming that he, rather than the King or Duke, *owns* Jim. Buried in the lie of silent assertion, hidden or muted but expressed in the silence, is the recognition that Huck has not the power to free Jim, that his act at best postpones the question of how to help Jim gain his dream of freedom. Yet when Huck recalls the incident of writing and tearing up his letter and the experience of making his decision, the deeds become something more, owing to the pressure of Twain's silent guilt which is all the stronger for remaining tacit, repressed or compressed within the lie of silence. That pressure enforces the pressure of commitment afterward in memory which commemorates the decision made earlier on the river and strains to make Huck's tribute to Jim the governing vision of Huck's adventure. It becomes the willed commitment to a liberation never made explicit, a fulfillment enacted only in the voiced cadences of Huck's spoken, Twain's written, speech. Created in the lie is the will to make the action convincingly seem, and in the language to be, a commitment of the moral imagination beyond what Twain knows it was then in fact. *Mea culpa* (1885): Jim and all fellow creatures should be, but are not yet, free. Huck's lie like Tom's will be a lie but it must be a better lie than his. Huck's lie must not only hide a fact but generate a vision. The lie must be suspenseful and dramatic like Tom's, and, just as Tom's will dramatize his petty ingenuity and show of valor, Huck's must dramatize his own flawed heroism. But Huck's drama must survive, in the durable rhythm of human speech, Huck's own later betrayals of Jim on the Phelps farm. Huck's lying words must be better prose than Tom's. In sum, Huck's idiom and drama must have better style. And they do, notably in Chapter 31 where Huck makes his famous decision. The section opens with words whose recurring "I" sounds identify the protagonist of the drama and the high pitch of intensity to which his colloquial instrument is tuned:

So I was full of trouble, full as I could be; and didn't know what to do. At last I had an idea; and I says, I'll go and write the letter—and *then* see if I can pray. Why, it was astonishing, the way I felt as light as a feather, right straight off, and my troubles all gone. So I got a piece of paper and a pencil, all glad and excited, and set down and wrote:

That paragraph is followed by one of the most efficient letters in English. Huck says that he tore it up, but it appears, usually without so much as a crease or a hyphen, in every copy of the book, defining now and again, then and still, the imminence of Jim's betrayals:

> Miss Watson your runaway nigger Jim is down here two mile below Pikesville and Mr. Phelps has got him and he will give him up for the reward if you send.—Huck Finn.

The letter is followed by a long paragraph in which the conjunction "and," the word "time," and the floating "ing's" of present participles recapture what Huck has before betrayed and will betray again but commemorates in the "now" of memory:

> I felt good and all washed clean of sin for the first time I had ever felt so in my life, and I knowed I could pray now. But I didn't do it straight off, but laid the paper down and set there thinking—thinking how good it was all this happened so, and how near I came to being lost and going to hell. And went on thinking. And got to thinking over our trip down the river; and I see Jim before me, all the time, in the day, and in the night-time, sometimes moonlight, sometimes storms, and we a floating along, talking, and singing, and laughing. But somehow I couldn't seem to strike no places to harden me against him, but only the other kind. I'd see him standing my watch on top of his'n, stead of calling me, so I could go on sleeping; and see him how glad he was when I come back out of the fog; and when I come to him again in the swamp, up there where the feud was; and such like times; and would always call me honey, and pet me, and do everything he could think of for me, and how good he always was; and at last I struck the time I saved him by telling the men we had small-pox aboard, and he was so grateful, and said I was the best friend old Jim ever had in the world, and the *only* one he's got now; and then I happened to look around, and see that paper.

Taut, brief sentences, with clipped "t" sounds and "x's," then define the final crisis:

> It was a close place. I took it up and held it in my hand. I was a trembling, because I'd got to decide, forever, betwixt two things, and I knowed it. I studied a minute, sort of holding my breath, and then says to myself:
> "All right, then, I'll *go* to hell"—and tore it up.
> It was awful thoughts, and awful words, but they was said. And I let them stay said; and never thought no more about reforming.

And so *Huckleberry Finn* got banned by fish-belly whites in Concord, Massachusetts, where there are or were people skinned in white who do not want their children to know about young Huck Finn, his forged integrity, his charged language and grammatical errors, and the vision burgeoning in his ripe adolescence. And the book more recently has been forced off the required reading lists in New York City, at the University of Massachusetts, and in Deland, Florida, at the insistence of collegians skinned in black who do not see, created in the antics of the Negro Jim, the aspirations of a people and the stature of a man. And we, with our fool imaginations, carry the burden of this lying fiction still as we translate it in our rereadings of it, moved in imaginings if not in undoubted deeds, to set these freedoms free.

NOTES

1. Hemingway's memory was somewhat blurred, since the two "boys" were not together when Jim was sold in Chapter 31, nor when Jim was recaptured as recounted in Chapter 42. Hemingway's linking of Huck and Tom, however, the implication that they owned the Negro "stolen" from them, and his incorporation of the term *nigger* in Jim's name ("Nigger Jim") display ways in which readers are implicated in the action of *Huckleberry Finn*. See *The Green Hills of Africa* (New York: Scribner's [1935] 1963), p. 22.

2. See Henry Nash Smith, *Mark Twain: The Development of a Writer* (Cambridge, Mass.: Harvard University Press, 1962), pp. 113–37, and his recent *Democracy and the Novel: Popular Resistance to Classical American Writers* (New York: Oxford University Press, 1978), pp. 104–27; and Leo Marx, "The Pilot and the Passenger: Landscape Conventions and the Style of *Huckleberry Finn*," *American Literature* 28 (1956): 129–46, and his *The Machine in the Garden: Technology and the Pastoral Ideal in America* (New York: Oxford University Press, 1964), pp. 319–41.

3. *The Colloquial Style in America* (New York: Oxford University Press, 1966), pp. 11, 20.

4. Morris argues the dangers of nostalgia in *The Territory Ahead* (New York: Harcourt and Brace, 1958), passim, but finds that what Huck lost "in the wilderness of his nostalgia" was recaptured by Twain "in this lucid moment of reminiscence and craft," p. 88.

5. "Forty or Fifty Years Ago," the notation on the title page, places the action between 1835, the year of Twain's birth, and 1845. In Chapter 40, Jim's determination to wait out a doctor for Tom even if it takes forty years would project the action ahead into the decade of 1875–1885 when Twain was writing the book.

6. James insisted that the best fiction, as in Zola, Scott, and Balzac, functions

as both novel and romance, which are "different sorts and degrees" of the same fictive undertaking, in the New York Edition's Preface to *The American* (New York: Scribner's, 1909). See *The Art of the Novel*, ed. Richard P. Blackmur, (New York: Scribner's, 1934), p. 31. Hawthorne's statement appears in a letter of November, 1850, quoted in James T. Fields, *Yesterdays with Authors* (Boston: Houghton, Mifflin, [1871] 1900), p. 56.

7. Quotations are from *The Writings of Mark Twain*, Author's National Edition, 25 vols. (Hartford, Conn.: American, 1899–1907), 20: 364–70, and 23: 161.

8. Comparable instances occur earlier but have no relation to the narrative structure of the book. In Chapter 31 the Duke cuts off in mid-sentence his disclosure of Jim's whereabouts, but Huck already knows it. In Chapter 27, during the Wilks affair, Huck keeps quiet about the King's fraudulent sale of the Wilks' slaves on the probably sanguine grounds that the fraud will be exposed and that "the niggers would be back home in a week or two."

FIVE

COTTON MATHER'S CRAZED WIFE
Mitchell Robert Breitwieser

> AB AMICO SATIS ADULATORE
> ON COTTON MATHER
>
> For *Grace* and *Art* and an Illustrious *Fame*
> Who would not look from such an Ominous Name?
> Where *Two Great Names* their Sanctuary take,
> And in a *Third* combined, a *Greater* make.
>
> Too gross flattery for me to transcribe;
> (tho' the poetry be good.)
>
> Cotton Mather, *Diary*.[1]

GENEALOGY is a frequent, familiar, and probably inescapable theme in discussions of Cotton Mather's life and work. But the metaphorical importance of filial responsibility as a structuring idea in other apparently unrelated departments of Mather's career is a topic only hinted at. I would like to begin such an examination with a quotation from his diary about *delight*. The bearing of delight on the argument at hand may not be conspicuous until it is remembered that delight is a necessary but profoundly problematic constituent element of dynastic ambition.

Cotton Mather's Crazed Wife

Cotton Mather's forty-fourth birthday in the mild early March of 1706 afforded him the opportunity to note the evidences of God's beneficence spread serenely around him in the profuse world of generation:

> I see all creatures everywhere full of their Delights. The birds are singing; the fish are sporting; the Four-Footed are glad of what they meet withall; the very Insects have their satisfactions. 'Tis a marvellous display of infinite goodness. The Good God has made his creatures capable of delights: He accomodates them with continual Delights. These Delights are the Delicious Entertainments of His infinite Goodness. His Goodness takes pleasure in the Delights of His creatures.—Well: Is there no way for me to Resemble and Imitate this Incomparable Goodness of God? Yes: I see my Neighbours all accomodated with their various delights. All have some and some have many. Now I may honestly make their delights my own . . . I may make their prosperity, not my *Envy*, but my *Pleasure* . . . Oh, the glorious Joy of the Goodness! Lord, Imprint this thy image on me![2]

Mather had had a similiar pause twenty years earlier on the morning before his first marriage, to Abigail Phillips. Afraid that the imminent relief from pent desire might cause him to forget the divine source of delight, he deliberately meditated so that he would not forget the purpose of the marriage-bed in the theological design: sons. His overview of delight in the 1706 birthday meditation shows the same concern; the proliferation of delight in nature is the surface-movement of deeper plans. During these same years, European natural historians were beginning to scan the field of genuses and species for structural identities and differences. The way was opening for Buffon and Cuvier. Mather's vision, by contrast, although equally attentive and perspicacious, is clearly retrospective, almost medieval.[3] For Mather, formal similarities of structure are only superficial and serve at best as preliminary, partial intuitions of the more profound analogies and sympathies sown in nature by the maker. Nature, to Mather, is a *variably expressive medium* and thus never sufficient in itself for the rigorously inquisitive mind. Mather was one of the first colonials admitted to the Royal Society, and his vigorous advocacy of the smallpox innoculation in the face of hostile public opinion shows that he was far from being a complete obscurantist in scientific matters. But he held rationalism to be a subordinate component of his thought, a mere preliminary phase in the investigation of divine patterning; all of Mather's thought is framed by an epistemological paradigm which, although it attempts to accomodate, is, finally, foreign to Enlightenment rationalism and its Unitarian manifestations in theology.

His birthday meditation emphasizes the reliability of vision. The image of God's will is visible in the delights of his creatures. Nature transparently shows the founding intention behind, and wisdom is the payoff for simple passive perception. But this passage from the diary represents an occasional, even rare, mood of Mather's. We cannot abstract his grovellings before the Lord or his fears of obtuse irrelevence, his self-excruciations or his wrestlings with doubt from this innocent wish to join in the frolic. He hesitates to trust prematurely; a reading of the diary leads one to conclude that the birthday meditation is a pacific interlude in an otherwise turbulent and anxious life. Or, put differently, Mather was by no means secure in the idea that natural signs or images immediately revealed their divine content to any passerby. Here, it is true, he simply *sees* the working of God's plan. But, it must be remembered, he did not condone the primary, unmediated, ecstatic intuitionism of the Antinomians. Signs are not simply seen. They must be *read*,[4] and the minister's canonized exegetical tradition, empowered by ecclesiastical polity, vigorously suppressed the possible vagaries of individual interpretation. Mather allowed himself the happy belief in appearances as a birthday present, but he did not fundamentally trust it. Fourteen years earlier, he had cautioned the court of Oyer and Terminer that a profane image or *spectre* of a man did not guarantee the profanity of that man's soul, and thus was not sufficient evidence for conviction of witchcraft. The issue of spectral representation is one manifestation of Mather's belief that, although God does express himself in the world, the world is a variably expressive medium *by design*. The intellectual movement from surface to depth, from the sign to its divine semantic substratum, had to be made with care guided by ecclesiastical dogma and even then could not attain to certainty. The attempt to represent the foundations of the world and history in a mental construct such as the *Magnalia Christi Americana* was marked by devout approximation and a reverence for real mysteries. Mather never forgot the inherent shortcomings of inquiry and, in his strong moments, did not despair over them. With Augustine, he argued that the world's apparent transparency was a potential trap for anyone naive enough to take it at face value. Augustine said that beauty was given to the unholy as well as the holy, and argued therefrom that visible signs were not sufficient evidence. The same is true of "delight" in Mather's birthday meditation; sin can be delightful, and a simple trust of appearances is idolatry or fetishism, mistaking the creature for its creator. Vision must be supplemented by a minister's critical faculty; one must read as well as see, read in a certain directed way, even if the text can never be perfectly deciphered before time's end.

This is the semiotic dimension of some sound and familiar learning about Puritanism. It is the application of the contention that the Puritan was "in the world but not of it," or of the assertion that Covenant orthodoxy was a mixture of rational belief in a revealed god with faith in an obscure god, to a theory of signs. For the Puritan, the world is a variably expressive medium. Reason's access to truth through signs was founded on an irrational and eleemosynary election of a few. The inscrutable origin of election set a limit on vision and knowledge during the period of profane history. Even to the elect, the world offered only glimmers and traces of its meaning. These were sufficiently secure to found a moral code and a culture, but they did not perfectly reveal their content to the understanding. The sign, in other words, proffered an apparent meaning and contained a divine meaning. The semiotic function of the doctrine of original sin was to explain the fact that, after Eden and before Apocalypse, the two orders could not converge.[5] Original sin, then, metaphorically, worsened sight; the devil, as Mather says, blinds men. The exit from Eden necessitated the supplement of ministerial exegesis. Between apparent and divine meaning, original sin opened a gap of variable distance, narrowed asymptotically by ministerial exegesis and widened by Satan's simulacra, apparent meanings which deliberately *eclipse* divine meaning.

The elect were those chosen to narrow the gap of meaning signalled by the concept of original sin. Grace implied the obligation to display truth in the medium of mundane, variably expressive languages. It existed in the elect as a potential for truth-telling coupled with an obligation to be sown, risked, or spent in hopes of adequate representation, the approach of truth to lucidity. This *dialectic* of expenditure underlies Mather's book *Bonifacius; or, Essays to Do Good*. *Bonifacius* lists the preeminent types of grace such as riches, learning, or civic talent and argues that each must be invested in the holy community. The eventual result, Mather argues, will be the increase of the community's spiritual health and the concomitant good name of the investor—both of which are visible public representations of a formerly inward and latent grace. Hoarding of grace, then, would be a spiritual deficiency: "But, alas! How much of the silver and gold of the world is buried in hands, where it is little better than conveyed back to the mines from whence it came! How much of it is employed to as little purpose as what arrives at Hindoostan, where a great part of it is, after some circulation, carried as to a fatal centre, and by Moguls lodged in subterraneous caves, never to see the light again."[6]

The reasons for hoarding, however, were all too apparent to Mather. Spiritual investment risked grace on the postlapsarian world, the domain of precarious perilous media that were easy prey to the devil's power to waylay and mislead through misrepresentation. The payoff is not to be taken for granted: "Misconstruction is one thing against which you will do well to furnish yourselves with the armour both of prudence and patience; prudence to prevent it, patience to endure it. You will be unavoidably put upon doing many good things, *which other people will see but at a distance*, and be unacquainted with the motives and the methods of your doing them; yea; they imagine their own purposes crossed in what you do; and this will expose you to their censures." (italics mine)[7] Satan, the origin and the exploiter of original sin, and his deputies such as envy, self-interest, or lust, are the personifications, the *name*, of the abysmal empty space between apparent and real meaning. Mather's battle with Satan is preeminently semantic. Before eyes are free of tears at history's end, ministers must supplement faulty vision with trusty signification. This essay will examine sexuality and writing, two media which Mather risked—sons who he hoped would uphold the family name and books, the true and holy representations of his own inner grace—and the demonic dissimulating interferences which shadowed his lifelong project.

The dialectical investment of grace which supplements and refurbishes the eminence of the past is the structuring idea behind Mather's attitudes toward sexuality and progeny. His self-set task as father was to stabilize and maintain the meaning (or reputation) of the name *Mather* against all mundane interruptions. The man sows or invests his grace in a medium of expression, woman; the result, a holy son, refills the signifier *Mather* with its elected meaning. But the medium is always a type of the first errant, Eve, and thus variably venal and sacred by definition. Prey to seduction and corruption (and, as we shall see, the madness which is the loss of the Lord's light), women, although not the origin of error, are the weak point at which the devil can enter and disrupt the sequence of sons fulfilling fathers.

The problem of misrepresentation perturbed Mather in his personal life when it upset his envisioned domestic order. Remember his own genealogy. His grandfathers, John Cotton and Richard Mather, and his father, Increase, were prominent New England divines who had been conspicuously successful in New England colonial policy. The period that Perry Miller calls "The Great Declension" may or may not be an historical fact; it existed, however, for Cotton Mather as a fear of personal shortcoming, a failure of the Mather name illuminated in juxtaposition with the brilliance of his dynastic precursors. The crucial central role of the minister in the community meant that New England's decline was the decline of the Mathers. The typological importance of the conjunction of the names Cotton and Mather ("Where *two great names* their sanctuary take . . .") did not escape him. The combination of surnames signalled him as the point at which the successes of the New England past converged, as the transumptive scion in which the sowing of the fathers was to have borne fruit. Hence his lifelong concern with what "Mather" *meant* to Boston, the community being the best available testimony of holiness. The sacred series of amazing victories narrated in *Magnalia Christi Americana* is the story of New England religion in general, but it tells that story synecdochically by narrating the exemplary lives of Mather's ancestors and their colleagues. Prophetic alienation and jeremiads are only appropriate in profane communities. In the holy community, the piety of the priest is both exemplary *to* and exemplary *of* the life of his flock. The decline in public recognition of the Mathers, therefore, meant a falling away from communal unanimity possibly based on the failure of those responsible for maintaining holy unanimity.

The sermon, Mather writes in *Paterna*, is composed of a doctrinal section, usually a Biblical citation, followed by an application of that text to the contemporary life of the congregation. The structure of the sermon is the structure of the past and the present, the father and the son. Successfully invested grace becomes a monument or text to be continually updated and thereby revitalized in the next genealogical moment. The dependence of application on doctrine is obvious; more subtly, doctrine is also dependent on continual citation in new circumstances. The past valorizes the present, but it also assigns the present the duty of active memory. In his turn, Cotton Mather was obliged to reproduce the family's ecclesiastical fervor by continuing the work of the past through the present and into the future. He would satisfy the demands of the present as minister and exegete; he would satisfy the demands of the future sexually and pedagogically, by supplying another Mather to apply the text of Cotton Mather's life. *Paterna* would then become a new chapter of *Magnalia Christi Americana*.

The son's duty was to re-present his father, restoring and reviving what time and the devil diminish. He must vindicate by repeating. Mather illustrates this in *Magnalia Christi Americana* when he celebrates Winthrop's son: "The son of Scipio Africanus proved a degenerate person and the *people* forced him to pluck off a signet-ring which he wore with his father's face engraven on it. But the son of our celebrated Governour Winthrop, was on the other side so like unto his excellent father for wisdom and virtue. . . ."[8] He continues by saying that Winthrop Jr. deserved the family name. Mather's figure is revealing. A name as much as an image on a ring is the visible sign of the father that the son bears with him, reminding him of the obligation to repeat in the present what was done in the past. The son is thereby a rebirth of a transpersonal, extratemporal unity, the elected family, of which the specific individual is only one moment. This has special meaning for Cotton Mather, named with patronyms. The son is a link, a member of a larger body. The only originality or specificity permitted him is, in the spirit of Puritan meliorism, to do the same thing better: "It was a problem among the ancient philosophers, 'Whether a child may not confer more benefits on his father than he has received from him?' This hath been sometimes bravely determined in the affirmative among us, when fathers have by the means of their own children been born again."[9]

The figures of rebirth and the signet-ring underscore Mather's belief that the son must be an image, resemblance, or representation of his father within the dictates of the genealogical imperative. The doubling of father by son is the tenor for the vehicle of the signet-ring: the stamped image on the ring is a metaphor for the impression left on each generation by its predecessors in a spiritual linkage of souls from first father to last son which vindicates the family and redeems the catastrophe of time that began when Adam fell. The reciprocal supplementation of father by son was not just one of the many metaphors that God had built into the world under the Covenant; it was a central one: the assurance that right interpretation of all the other covenanted signs would continue and increase on the way to the New Jerusalem. The sacred importance of a stable ministerial dynasty emerged as the organizing principle of *Magnalia Christi Americana,* which critics have often characterized as ancestor worship. Perry Miller calls the work "a sustained chant to the glory of mighty and already misty ancestral heroes."[10] According to Sacvan Bercovitch, "In the broadest sense, Mather's organizing principle is generational."[11]

Metaphor, then, is the structuring idea of genealogy; synecdoche figures the synchronic ensemble of the community of the elect, enabling an exemplary life to stand in for the total life of the community at that moment; and metaphor figures the life of the community in time, subordinating the difference between past and present beneath the solidarity of father and son, the "historeme" which is the atom of larger temporal continuities.

Metaphors, however, are often unstable with respect to the differences that they subordinate; the repetition of the same is hierarchically valorized above the extrinsic difference which it sublates. But the authority for this subordination, the Covenant, is inscrutable and eleemosynary, and difference waits the chance to escape its subordinate place and irrupt at the heart of continuity. The division between citation and application in the sermon may only be a rhetorical pause, but it might also be a fault or flaw, an abysmal gap across which the present can only measure ironically its hopeless difference from the past. The metaphor of father and son within the dynasty seeks to exile the difference between father and son to the domain of extrinsic, inessential contingency. But Mather, during the course of his life, was forced to admit the existence of troubling, conspicuous differences between himself and his eldest son.

Like most Puritan autobiographies, Mather's *Paterna* was written not as realistic self-description, but as lesson. Its title, a pun on *Paternal* and *Pattern,* adumbrates its central project of converting life into text to be cited and then applied—a preservation and readying of the author's life for that time when the present becomes past to be appropriated and faithfully supplemented by a new present. The book was conceived and begun as an epistle to Mather's oldest son Increase, a synecdoche for New England's future; it was finished with a dedication to another son, Samuel. That change is a sign of one of the nodal dramas of Mather's life.

Around 1715, Mather began to suspect that his eldest son, Increase, was not at all interested in prolonging the sacred tradition of the Mather ministers. Cotton Mather's diary reveals the growing dismay he felt in response to young Creasy's indifference to religious education. His doubts that he had failed as a son were strengthened when it looked as if he had failed as a father. Episodes in Creasy's wild career are narrated: he neglects his education; he goes out at night with 'gangs'; and, finally, he is accused of siring a bastard, the utmost horror to a dynastic purist like his father:

(Nov. 5, 1717) The Evil that I greatly feared is come upon me. I am within these few hours astonished with an Information, that an Harlot big with a Bastard, Accuses my poor son Cressy, and Lays her Belly to him. The most sensible judges, upon the strictest Enquiry, beleeve the youth to be Innocent. But yett, oh! the Humiliation!—Oh! Dreadful Case! O sorrow beyond any that I have met withal! What shall I do for the foolish youth! What for my Afflicted and Abased family![12]

Relief is the immediate tone of this entry, since Creasy was publicly absolved, allowing his father to suppose that the name was still recuperable, i.e., could still attain to a respectable public representation. But the deeper despair over the decline of the ministerial tradition also shows through. If sexuality is for prolonging a dynastic intention, then a bastard is a waste of seed and (like Edmund in *King Lear*) a cosmic irritant.

Cotton Mather fathered fifteen children. Four of them survived him. (Increase was lost at sea, appropriately.) Samuel did become a minister and was a friend of Franklin's. But even a Mather apologist like Barrett Wendell concedes that Samuel was a lukewarm minister at best, exemplar of a tradition watered down to the point where it could be co-opted by Franklin's worldly ethic. All of Cotton Mather's hopes for a restoration of faith were invested in Increase. He was the appointed heir of the Mather saintliness, the designated representation of their special election. The failure of Cotton Mather's genealogical ambitions was more testimony to the epidemic of misrepresentation in Massachusetts, and Increase's profligacy was consistently attributed to the devil's designs against Cotton Mather. Mather felt himself to be the victim of a personal attack. As are all heavenly representations, the son as image was separated from the father as original by a gap—desire.

Desire unmediated by divine aspirations was worldliness: the father and son were both tempted to be of the world as well as in it by the siren-song of delights to be indulged for their own sakes. For Mather, desire had to be transmuted and directed by transcendental aims; it could be enjoyed, but not entirely as an end in itself. Sexuality existed to further a genealogy of sons doubling fathers. To have a son was to gamble one's elected seed on a woman and to worry that the fledgling son might lose sight and wander from the father's imperative.

That the devil's work is to tempt men to indulge in desire for its own sake is a theological truism: the multitude of places where Mather located the devil working to strip desire of its transcendentality is amazing. He constructed an enormous intellectual machine to rationalize desire and combat its excesses. The antitypes in his symbolism are Eve and the Prodigal Son, both seduced by the world from their duty to God and Father. The first crime of woman necessitated a genealogy of the Elect because it brought death (hostile temporality) into the world. Instead of one immortal Adam, there had to be an immortal *series* of mortal men, a line of perishables that would collectively approximate one immortal. Since that first crime, women have systematically (the system given to them by the devil) conspired to disrupt genealogical representation by distracting fathers and seducing sons. Mather was highly suspicious of women for this one reason: since Eve, they have persisted in repeating the crime. The repetition which the father seeks to secure, in other words, is dogged by a shadowy double—the repetition of seduction, violation, distraction.

Women take the blame. In the episode of Creasy's seduction, remember, blame was laid on the "harlot big with bastard" for accusing Creasy of a crime for which he was exonerated. But the damage was done. This sounds a familiar note; the harlot misrepresented a Mather to the community. The son is only guilty insofar as he is unfledged and not yet familiar with the ways in which his holy image can be perverted by the devil's women.

In an article on Anne Hutchinson and *The Scarlet Letter*, Michael J. Colacurcio mentions Mather's "theological antifeminism."[13] As Colacurcio notes, Mather's most vehement statements on women occur in the section of *Magnalia Christi Americana* which concerns his grandfather John Cotton and Anne Hutchinson: "(Hutchinson) set up weekly meetings at her house, whereto threescore or fourscore people would resort, that they might hear the sermon's of Mr. Cotton repeated, but in such a sort that after the repetition, she would make her explicatory and applicatory declamations, wherein what she confirmed of the sermons must be *canonical*, but what she omitted all *Apocrypha*."[14] Hutchinson split her theology into aberrant applications that distorted the cited text. As I noted above, the relation of citation to application parallels the relation of son to father. The analogy becomes clear: heresy is a bastard. Hutchinson's sins as told in *Magnalia Christi Americana* are twofold. She perverted Cotton's truths, repeating them with a slight heretical difference, and she was licentious, having born several illegitimate children until she was providentially killed by Indians while in exile. The two motifs, intellectual heresy and sexual promiscuity, are so tightly interwoven in this chapter that they are finally indistinguishable. Mather implies that antinomianism, a compilation of "scandalous, dangerous and *enchanting* extravagancies,"[15] is the bastard son of a Cotton sermon, analogous to the "Monstrum, horrendum, in forme, ingens" which Hutchinson bore before her death:

It had no head: the face was below the breast: the ears were like an ape's, and grew upon the shoulders; the eyes and mouth stood far out; the nose was hooking upwards; the breast and back were full of short prickles, like a thorn-back; the navel, belly, and the distinction of sex, which was female, were in the place of the hips; and those back-parts were on the same side with the face; the arms, hands, thighs and legs, were as other childrens; but instead of toes, it had on each foot three claws, with taleons like a fowl: upon the back above the belly it had a couple of great holes like mouths; and in each of them stood out a couple of pieces of flesh; it had no forehead, but above the eyes it had four horns; two of above an inch long, hard and sharp; and the other two somewhat less.[16]

Earlier, I noted that the only originality permitted a son was to redo the father's work better. Here, Hutchinson's monster stands as a horrifying yet fascinating image of Mather's supreme distrust of the new, the original, and the extravagant, and the occult dangers they pose for one insistent on strict and faithful repetition of truth and family. Cotton's bout with the modern Eve and Creasy's interlude with the harlot are successive types of the first temptation.

Desire and women (who succumb to Satan at the drop of a hat, who need to be watched, indeed whose function for Mather was to be pliant and yielding) pose serious problems in Mather's symbolism. Before marrying his third wife, he was courted by an aggressive woman. Her importunate attentions caused some unpleasant stories to circulate in town about the audiences Mather granted her in his library (the same room where he sometimes secretly abased himself before the Lord, ashamed in his sin). The diary reveals that he was greatly relieved when she left off the pursuit and publicly testified that his behavior had been nothing but the most strictly honorable. But that was only a respite. The scandalous insanity of his third wife would once more endanger his image in the public eye and lead him back to self-doubts during those moments when he was alone with God. Because the Puritan was in a world of hostile time, he needed a woman for his commitment to sacred history and genealogy. They were a risk that had to be taken. Women and the desire that brings them to the Puritan's attention were dangerous, a risk that made the investment almost a gamble. They had to be tamed, their promiscuity overcome, and their issue directed to transcendental aims, just as the difference in metaphor is subordinated and sublated by the central repetition of the same. But it was equally possible that they might render the investment waste, leading the men by the nose, seducing father and son from the great resolve and zeal: " 'Tis noted of seducers that, like their father the devil, the old, the first seducer, they usually have a special design upon the *weaker sex*, who are more easily *gained* themselves, and then are fit instruments for the gaining of their husbands unto such *errors* as will cause them to *lose* their souls at last."[17]

All of the vagaries, insubordination, frailty and promiscuity with which sexuality was fraught for Mather had parallels in the dangers and risks of being an author. His commitment to writing was astounding. Including sermons and pamphlets, his published works number between four and five hundred. In *Phaedrus*, Socrates excoriates writing because it insistently repeats the same statement forever and thereby leads away from living memory. Suspicious as he was of spontaneous theologies such as antinomianism, Mather valued writing for the stubbornness which Socrates dismissed. Writing (or, more accurately, a book), to use the terminology of *Magnalia Christi Americana*, was *act* become *monument*, a persistent formal structure that compels its medium, language, to articulate the truths of Covenant election and theocratic dogma. The book is grace textualized and memorialized. It can therefore enforce a continuing truth in a world marred by temptation and death. Books do what sons should— they fastidiously revive-in-repeating the prior.[18] In *Magnalia Christi Americana*, Mather says that the glory of New England was signalled by three roughly contemporary events: the Reformation, the opening of the New World for European colonization, and the "resurrection of literature" through the invention of printing. Writing, especially for Mather but also for the Puritans in general, was not thought of as an enterprise ancillary to preaching and the government of theological aberrancies.[19] Even a casual reading of *Bonifacius* will show that Mather relished the conjunction of two meanings in the word *essay*. The word signified both a literary genre and the activity of "doing good." The coincidence of noun and active verb pleased him: in his career, primary activity and reflection in writing were not disjoined. Writing was in the world and did things. It was an active gesture necessary for the maintenance of faith. Alongside and on a par with the church and the university, writing books was an institution for the proper, adequate, and public representation of truth. The minister's books presented and defended right interpretation and thereby helped to bridge the semantic gap in the Covenant.

Perry Miller sketches an interesting correspondence when he speaks of Mather's "monstrous lust for publication." Mather's attitude toward the books he published was clearly paternalistic. They were his sons, conceived in an unruly medium and sent forth in the world to further truth. They would survive him. Language, however, like woman, existed in the ambiguous space between the world and God. It could either be disciplined to speak truth or it could become a crazed wife, stealing, seducing and perverting, leading the writer into fiction, fable, or myth.[20] Mather called *Magnalia Christi Americana* a "christianography," seeking to differentiate it from heretical American mythographies such as the blasphemous story of an Exodus of Mexican Indians which he reluctantly recounts in *Wonders of the Invisible World*.[21] Language is prey to the devil, a notoriously fine orator, because of its feminine indeterminacy. The author, like the father or the minister, may be tempted to give up the task when he finds his books misread and his reputation impugned. But that is the miser's refusal of risk. The author's gamble must be taken if truth is to go out and increase.

In 1700, in London, Robert Calef published *More Wonders of the Invisible World*. A rationalist criticism of the confusion of superstition, venery, and law in the Mathers' behavior during the witch trials, the book implicitly critiques theocracy in general, and a reader as perspicacious as Mather would not have misunderstood the implied attack on his own comprehensive world-view. Significantly, Calef's salvoes against the Mather way were directed not so much against the Mathers' behavior and its constituent ideas, but against the books that gave it expression. Calef seems to have realized that books and writing were fundamental to the Mather project. *More Wonders of the Invisible World* was not, directly, a response to Cotton Mather at Salem, but to Mather's representation of Mather at Salem in *Wonders of the Invisible World*. Calef's book questions the methods and motives whereby life-experience is autobiographized as exemplum. It was a battle of the books concentrating on the representational distance between "what really happened" and what the theocrat made of it in his book. *More Wonders of the Invisible World* was a counterbook, a near-namesake or rebellious son that doubled its father satirically by the addition of a single ironically hyperbolical word to the title. Barrett Wendell notes that Mather was troubled not only by what the book said and how it was received, but also by the fact that Calef was able to find a publisher. The invention of the press heralded and enabled Puritan writing, but it also allowed profane books to penetrate the community and intervene against the work of holy authors. Writing's modern form, printing, like women, was variably expressive, given indifferently to both fidelity and promiscuity. Mather believed that material for the book had been given to Calef by Benjamin Colman, pastor of the rival early-Unitarian Brattle Street Church of Boston. To Mather, both Calef and Colman (and their publishing successes) were evidences of the declension. In 1700, Calef published his book, Mather was without luck searching for a publisher for one of his, and Colman came out with a book that Mather accused of being full of the "devices of Satan." This is strong language to use about a fellow minister, but one must remember how close

Mather felt heresy could be to truth in appearance and, consequently, how necessary it was to publicly distinguish them from each other. Increase Mather, according to one story, had Calef's book burned in Harvard square. The evidence suggests that Cotton Mather felt threatened by a devil's conspiracy, a proliferation of books pestering his own and misrepresenting his writing to the people. The publication of Calef's and Colman's books in the same year was a sign that "All the Adversaries of the Churches Lay their Hands together as if by Blasting of us they hoped utterly to blow up all."[22]

What did Calef say? Mather was troubled by the possibility that the declension of faith in the late seventeenth century was a personal failure. He feared that he was not continuing the sanctified labors of his ancestors with enough ardor and conviction. The books which fathered Mather's books were, in his recent past, the sacred tomes of Increase and Richard Mather and John Cotton. Behind those books stretched a tradition (or textual genealogy) that included Foxe, Calvin, and Eusebius. The genealogy of sacred texts ultimately traces back to the Bible, the ursprache of textuality. For Mather, all experience is immediately textualized and installed in the fabric of the tradition. *The Christian Philosopher* is a compendium not so much of observation as of written information about natural history. The written tradition joins all phenomena to an ancient exegetical canon, and the modern author's proper relation to the tradition is one of filial veneration:

But in these *Quotations*, there has been proposed, first, a due *Gratitude* unto those, who have been my *Instructors*; and indeed, *something within me* would have led me to it, if *Pliny*, who is one of them, had not given me a Rule; *Ingenuum est profiteri per quos profeceris* ("It is noble to acknowledge by whom you have profited."). It appears but a piece of *Justice*, that the *Names* of those whom the Great God has distinguished, by employing them to make those *Discoveries*, which are here collected, should live and shine in every such Collection.[23]

In this context, we may understand the gravity of Calef's critique of Mather's book-writing. He accused Mather of eclipsing the Biblical light with claptrap about witches instead of pursuing the task of re-presenting the Bible in a modern form, the project which underlies Mather's *Biblia Americana*. Calef argued, in Perry Miller's words, that "all learned theories concerning the nature of sin or its evidences are 'human invention'—mere 'traditions' foisted onto scripture on a par with the superstitions of Rome."[24] By assimilating *tradition* under the heading superstition, Calef inverted Mather's doctrinal belief in a tradition that *opposed* superstition and Catholicism. Calef's argument disturbs the whole structure of interpreting intrusions from the invisible world which John Winthrop called the "Holy Allegory" with which Mather shored up his enterprise.

Worse, by saying that Mather foisted superstition onto scripture, Calef as much as said that Mather helped erect the "thousands of blinds" that obstruct the transmission of the light of truth from the Bible. In essence, he accused Mather of aiding the devil. Foisting superstition onto the Bible amounted to breaking the generation of texts from the Bible to the present by saying something new, unfounded by divine sanction, and therefore heretical, instead of *repeating* the sacred in a modern form. Originality and innovation of too severe a degree were impermissible to a theology which could not tolerate the vagaries of language which shifted or altered divine meaning. The image which Calef made of Mather's book caused *Wonders of the Invisible World* to seem as if it had strayed from its fathers into the wilderness of heresy, superstition, fiction, or fantasy. Calef called *Wonders of the Invisible World* a "legend" and intimated that it might even be "direct blasphemy."[25]

Fiction, from the Puritan point of view, is a play within language for its own sake. It exploits the semantic gap of the postlapsarian world by creating formal structures without foundation in divine intention. Story (unless clearly signalled as allegory, as in *Pilgrim's Progress*, or unless presented as authentic history, such as the *Magnalia*) tended to be a dissimulating simulacrum, linguistic delight without reference to a transcendent absolute. Mather's comments on style in *Manuductio ad Ministerium* relieve the writer of a slavish obligation to Hooker's *plain style* which was a prescription to write in the style of the Bible and thus perpetuate the dynasty of sacred books. The result of the plain style, however, was more often tortuous grammatical constructions than real piety. Mather, in *Manuductio ad Ministerium*, argues that young ministers should adopt a freer style and allow themselves to cite pagan poets in order to be more rhetorically adept in educating modern congregations. But Mather also carefully reminds the reader that these must remain extrinsic and ornamental. They represent for him a kind of contagion which, used carefully, promotes the good but might also, unless kept under a vigilant eye, seduce the piety which must remain at the sermon's heart. The familiar ambivalence of cooperation and violation which Mather saw in women was also true of pagan references, a pleasing personal style, indeed rhetorical devices in general. The sermons of the minister are children of the Biblical tradition and must recognize their patrimony by representing the father-text. If they devolve into legend, superstition, stylistic self-absorption or pagan fabulation, they must, like the son of Scipio Africanus, be deprived of the ring on which is engraved the image of their father.

Believing as he did in the connection between legend and heresy, Mather was upset when Calef's book accused his of being a Romish fiction that obscured rather than revealed the Bible. The general worry that his books were liable to be misrepresented by a conspiracy of devil's advocates results in several striking passages in the diary. Because of the covenanted gap in meaning, falsehood is not necessarily perceived in its proper character and the emissaries of Satan can write and publish books. The devil can, through the accusations made in such books, erode the updating of the Bible that the minister seeks to enact. The devil will spawn counterbooks to impugn the good book. The central and most heinous of these counterbooks was a veritable anti-Bible circulated in Salem in search of signatures. Notice how, in the following passage, Mather suggests but does not elaborate upon an occult connection between this devil's book and his own personal authorial diligence:

I had filled my Countrey with little BOOKS, in several whereof, I had, with a Variety of Entertainment, offered the *New-Covenant* formally drawn up, unto my Neighbours: hoping to engage them eternally unto the Lord, by their subscribing with *Heart* and *Hand*, unto that *Covenant*. Now in the late horrid *Witchcraft*, the manner of the *Spectres* was to tender BOOKS unto a *League* with the *Divel* therein exhibited, and so become the *Servants* of the Divel forever; which when they refused, the *Spectres* would proceed to wound them with Scalding, Burning, Pinching, Pricking, Twisting, Choaking, and a thousand preternatural Vexations.[26]

Holy persuasion proceeds in mild blandishments, but the devil torments. But beneath this difference, Mather clearly sketches his theory of demonic textual doubling. The editor of the diary notes a similar passage from *Wonders of the Invisible World*: "While others have had their Names Entred in the *Devil's Book*; let our names be found in the *Church Book*."²⁷ The devil's assaults on Mather's credibility undermine the minister's position as spiritual leader. The attack can even be so cleverly done that the minister may doubt himself, an ever-present threat in a world whose meaning was never, by definition, immediately present to the faulty eyesight of historical man.

The anxiety over possible delusion seems to have preyed on Mather even while he was writing *Magnalia Christi Americana*. In one of the most eloquent passages in that book, he triumphantly announces that the Phoebus of Christianity has broken through the devil's clouds. Although the grounds of certitude are not presented, Mather writes that *Magnalia Christi Americana* is revealed truth despite all accusations. He clearly believes that the erection of a monument of truth such as the *Magnalia* is a victory analogous to the building of the Puritan city in the wilderness. The labyrinthine dodges and sophistries of language, like the entangled pathways of the American *selva oscura*, are a field of action, the page on which to write the name. A risk to be taken, these wildernesses offer the reward of an ever-increasing faith when mastered:

Reader, twas not unto a Delphos, but unto a Shiloh, that the planters of New-England have been making their progress, and King Phillip is not the only Python that has been giving them obstruction in their passage and their progress thereunto. But if *Infaelix Exitus Persecutorum* (fearful is the end of persecutors) is any note of the *true church*, I am sure New-England has a true church to people it; for all the *serpents*, yea, or giants, that formerly molested that religious plantation, found themselves engaged in a fatal enterprise. We have by a true and plain history secured the story of our success against all the Ogs in this *woody* country from falling under the disguises of mythology; but it administers to us the reflection which has often been made, that as of old the ruins that still overtook the persecutors of the poor Picardines caused men to say, "If a man be weary of his life, let him become an enemy to the Picardines!" The like ruins have overwhelmed them that have persecuted the poor New Englanders. And we will not conceal the *name* of the God our Saviour, as an heathen country sometimes would. . . . No, 'tis our Lord Jesus Christ, worshipped according to the rules of his blessed gospel, who is the great Phoebus, that "SUN of Righteousness," who hath so saved his churches from the designs of the "generations of the dragon."²⁸

The plantation of holiness in New England is opposed by political enemies such as King Phillip and by linguistic enemies such as the Ogs of mythologies. The New Englanders are planters, investors of the seed of grace in a hostile ground, beneficiaries not only of a holy community but of the power to articulate the pellucid truth of the gospel. The emergence from concealment into light is the dividend of holy labor.

What, then, if the written monument begins to seem wasted tribute, an expenditure of zeal that does not pay off? Investment in history is a gamble that the foundations of the mundane economy are not delusion. Mather took the gamble, staking his enterprise on a single rigid code of belief, a comprehensive perspective that surveyed widely different fields of investigation and structured them all with the paradigm of grace, investment, risk, indetermination, molestation, representation, and continuity. The energy to pursue the gambit, the anodyne for the fear of waste or irrelevent work, was the idea of an occulted antagonist. Mather believed that the devil not only pursued all good men but for some reason chose him in particular. Coincidence is the departure point for an epistemological strategy which centered on a paranoid trope that assimilates all frustration to a single cause, reveals a need to *elide* the fear of personal insufficiency by covering it with an hypostatic antagonist, an exact double in every sense but one—it mirrors by inversion, undoing everything the original tries to do. Men of tremendous energy and eschatological ambition are often possessed and, finally, bolstered, by the idea that their exceptionality attracts the attention of an inscrutable malignity. Throughout his life, Mather was convinced that he was shadowed by a devil trying to undermine the *magnalia matheriana.*

The consolation afforded by the demon-hypostasis failed him once, at a suggestive moment. In the diary of November, 1716, he reveals a startling discovery. Several earlier passages of "Good Devised" had been so completely crossed out that they were illegible and consequently lost to future readers. A "Good Devised," noted by G.D. in the margin, was an outstanding passage on which Mather focused special attention, pointing to it as a privileged moment when the recounting of daily experience was transmuted into an exemplary, monumental text. The "Good Devised" were nodes where the diarist penetrated the apparent meanings of his life and divined the real meaning beneath. The cancellation of several of these caused him consternation. "I could never learn How or Why the Blotts were made."[29] Figuratively, the erasure of these passages signifies the blotting of connection with the pattern/paternity underlying history. During his life, Mather believed that the holy significance of many deeds of good devising had been obscured by an invisible enemy. Especially his books (but also his attitudes towards his sons and his congregation) are evidence of Mather's dedication to the presentation of a lucid truth that seeks to explain the visible world in terms of invisible intentions, thereby anchoring the present in the monumental past and shaping an at least equally monumental future. But malignity blocked the fruition of this project and much of his self-examination hovered around the arcane origin of the blot. What was the source of molestation—personal shortcoming, Satan's calumny, God's whim, or the inherent inadequacy of the languages given the minister to make the best of?

Two years later, he discovered the source of the blotting of the Good Devised. His third wife had gradually gone quite mad and was now unwilling to respect his lifelong project. Content at first with crossing out Good Devised on the sly, her madness worsened until she delighted in stealing some of the diaries, found the opportunity to so, and then refused to return them. Playful perhaps, but then Mather's attitude toward play in ecclesiastical matters was hardly approving. Then, too, reason being the light of the Lord, insanity in his own house would hardly elicit benign tolerance. In his last years, Mather, like Voltaire, braved hostility to encourage the acceptance of innoculation against smallpox, a medical novelty that was, symbolically at least, dialectical, since it implied that the risk of a little contagion led to the reward of a greater health.[30] The intrusion of poison into his own house, even between the covers of his diary, however, was more than a healthy dose of risk. Mather could not help but notice and be fascinated by the fact that his wife's madness seemed to be not random caprice or general eccentricity, but instead a deliberate violation of his holy work. The conjunction of woman, madness, and an actual physical assault on the process of book-writing combines in an uncannily succinct way the maneuvers of diabolism. The origin of the blot was the wife gone mad, shedding the pleasant yoke of marital cooperation and violating holy ends. It is fascinating to note, if I may quote at length, what Mather makes of all this:

21 d. xim. 1718. Wednesday. My glorious Lord has inflicted a New and Sharp Chastisement upon me. The consort in whom I flattered myself with the View and Hope of an Uncommon Enjoyment, has dismally confirmed it unto me, that our *Idols* must prove our *sorrow*. Now and then, in some of the former years, I observed and suffered grievous outbreakings of her proud passions; but I quickly overcame them with my Victorious love, and in the Methods of Meekness and Goodness. And *O my Saviour, I ascribe unto Thee all the glory of it, and I wondrously praise Thee for it*; I do not know, that I have to the Day spoke one Impatient or Unbecoming word to her; tho' my provocations have been unspeakable; and it may be few men in the World, would have borne them as I have done. But this last Year has been full of her prodigious paroxysms, which have made it a year of such Distresses unto me, as I have never seen in my Life before. When the paroxysms are gone off, she has treated me still with a Fondness, that it may be, few Wives in the World have arrived unto. But in the Return of them (which of late grow more and more frequent) she has insulted me with such Outrages, that I am at a loss, which I should ascribe them to: Whether a Distraction which may be somewhat Haereditary, or to a possession (whereof the symptoms have been too direful to mention.) In some other papers I leave a more particular Account of these Things.[31] But what I have here to Relate is this: That She expressed such a Venome, against my Reserved Memorials, of experience in, and projection for, the Kingdom of God, as has obliged me to Lay the Memorials of this year, I thought, where she would not find them. It has been a year wherein I have made advances in piety, than in many former years. Perhaps my Journey thro' the Wilderness just expiring, I must ride more way in one year than in forty before. . . . Fore every Day I have noted, my purposes of Service for the Kingdom of God. For fear of what might happen, I have not one disrespectful word of this proud woman, in all the papers. But this week, she has in her indecent Romaging found them, and she not only detains them from me, but either she has destroy'd them, or she does protest, that I shall never see them any more. I have offered unto her, to blot out with her pen whatever she would not have to be there. But no loving entreaties of Mine can prevail upon her to Restore them. Only, she gives me hopes of restoring some time or other, the papers of the Four or Five preceding years, which the ungentlewomanly woman has also stolen. . . . I have lived for near a year in a Continual Anguish of Expectation, that my poor Wife, by exposing her Madness, would bring a Ruine on my ministry. But now it is exposed, my Reputation is marvellously preserved among the people of God, and there is come such a General and Violent Blast upon her own, as I cannot be troubled at. I will now go on.[32]

The passage begins with a consideration of the possibility that her madness is a punishment for Mather's idolatrous love and consequent forsaking of the genealogical mandate. It ends with the familiar cathartic expulsion of doubt after his exoneration in the public eye. It refuses to consider the possibility that her disobedience is a direct result of the severity and singlemindedness of the regime which she violates. Between the doubt at the beginning and the relief at the end, Mather's search for self-exculpation employs two concepts.

He stresses the insuperable periodicity of her outbreaks and the necessity of repeatedly taming her paroxysms with persuasion and of convincing her of the goodness of wifely propriety. The grace of the husband, in other words, is not expended once on woman and then allowed to rest. It must be continually reinvested, each time restoring and refurbishing the victorious persuasions of the past. The incessant renewal of caprice, and the consequent continuous necessity of vigilance, conflates in this passage with the interminable task of doing good in the community and with his reflection on years of ministerial activity. The process of expending grace can never rest or it will lapse. Each success becomes a monument or memorial but is not thereby sufficient; it has to be supplemented with new activity. The passage thus expresses Mather's weariness with the absence of permanence. He escapes guilt, in other words, by typing his wife's madness as a punishment of postlapsarian man, not of Mather. This thought then exalts him, because it means that, like Job, his *personal* innocence and piety have led God to choose him as the one in whom to test *man's* frailty, an examination which public acclaim assures him he has passed marvellously.

That is the conceptual working-out of self-doubt in this passage. Another note, however, remains—the radical indeterminacy of the origins of the wife's madness. He does not cast his wife, as he did Calef and Colman, with the generations of the dragon. On the topic of the cause of madness, there are speculations, multiple determinations, but, finally, silence and the less than exultant "I will go on." The source of the blot is the madwoman, the ungentlewomanly woman, but behind the madness is an interpretive knot that cannot be unravelled. Thought snarls: decisive insight into origins is reserved for God and man's repeated victories are always partial. He knew that he had attracted the attention of the invisible world, but his theology condemned him to not know absolutely where he stood in the pattern on which the world was founded. Despite his obsessively pertinacious labors, the "Methods of Meekness and Goodness," delirium found him.

NOTES

1. Cotton Mather, *Diary* (New York: Frederick Ungar, 1911), 1: 475.
2. *Ibid.*, p. 553.
3. See Otho T. Beall, Jr., and Richard H. Shryock, *Cotton Mather: First Significant Figure in American Medicine* (Baltimore: Johns Hopkins Press, 1954) for a good elucidation of the status of Mather's "medieval" science and its relation to its contemporary context.
4. See Cotton Mather, *The Christian Philosopher*, in Kenneth B. Murdock, ed., *Selections* (New York: Hafner, 1926), p. 286: "*Chrysostom*, I remember, mentions a *Twofold Book* of GOD, the Book of the *Creatures*, and the Book of the *Scriptures*. . . . We will now for a while read the *Former* of these Books, 'twill help us in reading the *Latter*: They will admirably assist one another. The Philosopher being asked What his *Books* were; answered *Totius Entis Naturalis Universitas*. ("The natural university of all the existing universe.") All Men are accomodated with that *Publick Library*. *Reader*, walk with me into it, and see what we shall find so legible there, *that he that runs may read it*. Behold a Book, whereof we may agreeably enough use the words of honest *Aegardus*; *Lectu hic omnibus facilis, esti nunquam legere dedicerint, et communic est omnibus, omniumque oculis expositus* ("Here is reading easy for everyone even though they have not learned to read, and it is open to all, and set out before everyone's eyes."). But the welter of citation and laborious interpretation in *The Christian Philosopher* suggests that the reading of the books in nature's library is not such an easy task. For instance, he suggests that earthquakes and volcanoes are the results of chemical reactions beneath the earth's surface. But they are also signs of God's wrath. One would have to scrutinize both the geochemical and the providential determinations of the occurence. Even then, the phenomenon would not have been exhaustively described: "But it's time to stop, we are got beyond *Human Penetration*; we have *dug* as far as 'tis fit any *Conjecture* should carry us. . . . It shall be then no indecent *Anticipation* of what should have been observed at the conclusion of this Collection, here to demand it of you, that you glorify the infinite Creator of this, and of all things, as *incomprehensible*. You must acknowledge that *Human Reason* is too feeble, too narrow a thing to comprehend the *infinite* God." (309–10). Any phenomenon—such as the madness of his third wife discussed at the end of my essay—is thus overdetermined, and the book of nature elaborately polysemous.
5. See *The Christian Philosopher*, pp. 313–14: "Go on my learned *Grew*, and maintain (who more fit than one of thy *recondite Learning*?) *that there is hardly any one thing in the World, the Essence whereof we can perfectly comprehend*. But then to the *natural Imbecillity* of REASON, add the *moral Depravations* of it, by our Fall from God, and the Ascendant which a corrupt and vicious *Will* has obtain'd over it, how much ought this Consideration to warn us against the Conduct of an *unhumbled Understanding* in things relating to the *Kingdom of God*?"
6. Cotton Mather, *Bonifacius; or, Essays to Do Good* (Boston: Lincoln and Edmands, 1808), p. 115. This book represents Mather at his least metaphysical, and it is more concerned with the homilies of civic virtue than it is with history

or the New World. It is no surprise that *Bonifacius* is among the books listed as favorites in Franklin's *Autobiography*. Stripped of much of its spiritual profundity, Mather's ethical imperative to invest grace reappears as Poor Richard's advice: "Remember that money is of the prolific, generating nature. Money can beget money, and its offspring can beget more, and so on. Five shillings turned is six, turned again it is seven and threepence, and so on, till it becomes a hundred pounds. The more there is of it, the more it produces every turning, so that the profits rise quicker and quicker. He that kills a breeding-sow, destroys all her offspring to the thousandth generation. He that murders a crown, destroys all that it might have produced, even scores of pounds," quoted in Max Weber, *The Protestant Ethic and the Spirit of Capitalism* (New York: Charles Scribner's Sons, 1958), p. 49. Mather's critique of hoarding is directed against Catholicism, monasticism and the *contemptus mundi* tradition; Franklin is merely chastening misers for their folly. In the abstract, however, both see investment as a para-procreative necessity and circulation as the realm of providential benificence, and therefore participate in the nascent ethics of capital. Compare the quotations above to the following from Marx: "This naive form of hoarding becomes perpetuated in those communities in which the traditional mode of production is carried on for the supply of a fixed and limited circulation of home wants. It is thus with the people of Asia [Mather's Hindoostan?], and particularly of the East Indies" *Capital* (New York: International Publishers, 1967), 1: 131. Also: "This boundless greed after riches, this passionate chase after exchange-value, is common to the capitalist and the miser; but while the miser is merely a capitalist gone mad, the capitalist is a rational miser. The never-ending augmentation of exchange-value, which the miser strives after, by seeking to save his money from circulation, is attained by the more acute capitalist, by constantly throwing it afresh into circulation" (1: 153). In response to Mather (to a certain extent) and especially to Franklin, one might quote Marx's terse dictum: "Circulation . . . begets no value" (1: 163).

7. *Bonifacius*, 16.

8. Cotton Mather, *Magnalia Christi Americana* (New York: Russell and Russell, 1967), 1: 158.

9. *Magnalia*, 2: 373.

10. Perry Miller, *The New England Mind: From Colony to Province* (Boston: Beacon Press, 1953), p. 135.

11. Sacvan Bercovitch, *The Puritan Origins of the American Self* (New Haven: Yale University Press, 1975), p. 130.

12. *Diary*, 2: 484.

13. Michael J. Colacurcio, "Footsteps of Anne Hutchinson: the Context of *The Scarlet Letter*," *English Literary History* 39, no. 3 (September 1972), 475.

14. *Magnalia*, 2: 517.

15. *Ibid.*, p. 518.

16. *Ibid.*, p. 519.

17. *Ibid.*, p. 516.

18. Mather's attitudes are an instance of what Jacques Derrida describes as the tension between writing and the book in Western metaphysics: "The idea of

the book, which always refers to a natural totality, is profoundly alien to the sense of writing. It is the encyclopedic protection of theology and of logocentrism against the disruption of writing, against its aphoristic energy, and, as I shall specify later, against difference in general" (*Of Grammatology* [Baltimore: Johns Hopkins University Press: 1974, 1976], p. 18).

19. A fascinating discussion of the Puritan preference for the printed word is the topic of chapter one of Larzer Ziff's *Puritanism in America* (New York: Viking Compass, 1973).

20. Puns, for instance. Mather's puns are frequent, and usually bad. Paternal and pattern combine in Paterna. Lodestone becomes lĕadstone and then lēadstone; man is magnetically led to God. But puns not impregnated with a correspondent semantic conjunction are examples of phonic promiscuity, false semblances that distract from orthodoxy.

21. Cotton Mather, *Wonders of the Invisible World*, in G. L. Burr, ed., *Narratives of the Witchcraft Cases* (New York: Charles Scribner's Sons, 1914), p. 245: " 'Tis very remarkable to see what an Impious and Impudent *imitation* of Divine Things is Apishly affected by the Devil, in several of those matters, whereof the Confessions of our Witches, and the Afflictions of our *Sufferers* have informed us. . . . The Devil which *there* thus imitated the Church of the *Old Testament* would Imitate the Affairs of the Church in the *New*. The *Witches* do say, that they form themselves much after the manner of *Congregational Churches*; and that they have a *Baptism* and a *Supper* among them, abominably Resembling those of our Lord." I have elided a long description of a group of Mexican Indians who imitated the Old Testament by going on a devilish copy of the Hebrews' Exodus.

22. *Diary*, as quoted in Barrett Wendell, *Cotton Mather: The Puritan Priest* (New York: Harbinger, 1963), p. 110. The publishing histories of Calef's and Colman's books is taken from pp. 109–10.

23. *The Christian Philosopher*, in Murdock, *Selections*, pp. 288–89.

24. *The New England Mind: From Colony to Province*, p. 250.

25. Robert Calef, *More Wonders of the Invisible World*, quoted in Milton R. Stern and Seymour L. Gross, eds., *American Literature Survey: Colonial and Federal to 1800* (New York: Viking Press, 1962), p. 147.

26. *Diary*, 1: 155.

27. *Ibid.*, p. 155n.

28. *Magnalia*, 2: 579.

29. *Diary*, as quoted in Wendell, p. 193.

30. The theory of smallpox innoculation mirrors perfectly the theory that rhetorical ornamentation and citations of pagan poetry are a sort of contagion with which the minister injects his sermon in hopes of an increase of persuasive power; see pp. 103–4 above, also *The Christian Philosopher*, in Murdock's *Selections*, p. 339: "What tho there are *venomous Plants*? An excellent *Fellow of the College of Physicians* makes a just Remark: '*Aloes* has the Property of promoting *Haemorrhages*; but this Property is good or bad, as it is used; a *Medicine* or a *Poison*; And it is very probable that the most dangerous *Poisons*, skilfully managed, may be made not only *innocuous*, but of all other Medecines the most *effectual*.' "

31. Wendell reports that the "More Particular Account" to which Mather alludes was either never written or else lost. See, however, Mather's theory of madness, or *balneum diaboli*, written two years after his wife's madness, in *"De Tristibus, or, The Cure of Melancholy,"* chapter XXV of The *Angel of Bethesda*, reprinted in Beall and Shryock, pp. 198–203.

32. *Diary*, 2: 583–84.

SIX
ON LITERATURE AND CONDENSATION: ROBERT MUSIL'S EARLY NOVELLAS
Peter Henninger

I PROPOSE to question the relation of literature and psychoanalysis by confronting it with the texts of a writer, Robert Musil, who recognized himself *as* a writer between 1897 and 1907, in the course of a process which was contemporary to the most crucial stages of Freud's discovery and exploration of the unconscious.

Musil's fame, today, is mainly founded on his monumental yet unfinished *Man without Qualities*. I will not deal with this work here. Nor will I say anything about his more popular books such as *Three Women* and very little about his early novel *Die Verwirrungen des Zöglings Törless* (translated as *Young Törless*). The texts I will be concerned with were, and still are, of all those published by Musil the most unsuccessful ones, although—and this may be of some importance—the author himself never lost interest in them and throughout his life continued reading and commenting on them in his diary and elsewhere. Two of the texts I am referring to were published in 1911 as Musil's second book, *Vereinigungen* (*Unions*). They are entitled "The Perfecting of Love" and "The Temptation of Quiet Veronica"; the third text, "The Enchanted House," goes back to 1908.[1]

What follows are extracts—although presented in different order and articulation—of a book entitled *Der Buchstabe und der Geist* (*The Spirit and the Letter*) to be published next year in Germany.

I shall now summarize (as far as possible) those three stories and at the same time retrace the circumstances in which they were written.

After he had published his novel *Törless*, which immediately attracted the attention of the prominent critics, one of the most important figures of what we would now call the literary establishment of that time in Germany, Franz Blei, asked Musil to contribute a shorter narrative to an international literary magazine he was about to found. Musil, who at that time was a student of philosophy and psychology at the University of Berlin, was on the point of finishing his thesis on Ernst Mach. He therefore could not fulfill Franz Blei's request immediately. It was only after he had received his Ph.D. degree in Berlin and had finished a brief period of military service in Austria, in May, 1908, that he began writing the novella which was subsequently published in the December issue of *Hyperion* under the title "The Enchanted House."

The story concerns a lieutenant in the army of the Austro-Hungarian Empire who happens to be quartered, during a maneuver, in the residence of a noble family, in a small provincial town. While preparing to leave this house for a few days, the young officer overhears a dialogue in the room adjacent to his, between a woman—a middle-aged yet unmarried lady, descendant of that family—and an unknown man who, unsuccessfully, declares his love to her. The point of view then switches to this couple and we learn that they agreed that the man should leave town the same night by train, travel south to the sea-shore and there commit suicide. After he has gone, the woman, whose name is Victoria, remains in a state of great agitation until the postman brings a letter from her lover saying that he has found his way back into life and no longer intends to kill himself. When a little later the lieutenant returns, Victoria literally throws herself at him, and they make love on the stairs leading up to his room. Strangely, Victoria then attempts to poison the *Oberleutnant* (a fact which is not mentioned at the end of the story but only in its very first sentence).

During the summer of 1908, while he was writing "The Enchanted House," Musil took note of a fantasy of jealousy—the sudden vision of the unfaithfulness of his friend and wife-to-be, Martha—which served him as basis for "The Perfecting of Love," a novella that he probably began writing in January or February, 1909, and did not complete until July, 1910. The protagonist of this story, Claudine, who lives harmoniously with her husband, takes a journey to visit her daughter, child of an adulturous relationship from the period of her first marriage. On her way to the mountains where her child is educated in a boarding-school, Claudine finds herself overwhelmed by her own past. On the train she meets a man traveling to the same destination who will reside in the same hotel and who tries to seduce her. The man, who turns out to be a high official, a *Ministerialrat*, courts her even more assiduously the next day, when because of the snow which has fallen during the night, it becomes impossible to leave the village. Claudine accepts the *Ministerialrat*'s advances and finally convinces herself that the adultery she commits with him can in some way consummate the love that binds her to her husband.

During the summer of 1910, probably before he had finished "The Perfecting of Love," Musil decided to publish the novella in a book together with a new version of "The Enchanted House," now entitled "The Temptation of Quiet Veronica." This proved to be more difficult than he had anticipated, and it was only after having written an intermediate version, which he gave up after a certain number of pages, that he managed to compose "The Temptation . . ." as it now figures in *Vereinigungen*. With regard to this definite text, an American critic, Burton E. Pike notes that "even upon repeated readings one cannot say precisely what *happens*."[2] In fact, it suffices to compare the story to "The Enchanted House" to discover that action as such has now altogether disappeared once the sexual act at the end of this novella has been expunged (although its trace—the meeting on the stairs—is still there). Moreover, the three protagonists, Veronica (the former Victoria) and the two men of opposing character (the "he"- and the "she"-man) with whom she is involved, are now supposed to be close relatives, probably cousins. And, at the end, the one who failed to commit suicide for Veronica is expected to join the other two again (and everything will be as before). Thus, instead of a proper action, one finds in this text only a series of anecdotal episodes, related in a non-chronological order. That is why the "plot" of this novella remains elusive, or as Pike puts it, why Musil "succeeds here only in being opaque."[3]

It is through a reading of these three stories, "The Enchanted House," "The Perfecting of Love," and "The Temptation of Quiet

Veronica," that I will investigate the relation or rather the different kinds of relations between the writing of fiction and the Freudian theory of the unconscious.

To begin, I will now quote from the first of these novellas, "The Enchanted House," a passage which comes in the beginning of the story. It describes what the lieutenant hears through the wall:

A deep female voice raised in passion on the verge of breaking cried out: "Leave me alone, I can't! I just can't!!" and her words split and crumbled like soggy bits of masonry. Then Demeter heard the man speak again: "But you love me nevertheless, you feel this in your whole being, you don't have a single thought from which I am absent, your life only began again with mine. Don't deceive yourself . . . this is love; tell me . . . you do love me, don't you. . . ?" And the woman's voice responded quieter than before but raising again to the breaking-point as she spoke: "Love you, I . . . perhaps, that is no . . . no, I don't know." And Demeter heard the man speak again: "Listen to me, Victoria, if you refuse, I will leave today and by tomorrow I will have thrown my life away, if you refuse. You know my life this last year has depended on you. I know that you love me and tomorrow, perhaps you will know it too: I am asking you once more, can you?" Then followed a short silence and then Demeter heard a "no!" and then "no!!" again, uttered twice like a whip or an insensate clinging and then, once again, "no," softer, exhausted and like a pang of remorse. (*PSt*, p. 147)

A formal description would establish that in this passage direct speech alternates with indirect speech and that we have five segments of direct speech, five utterances, three attributed to the woman, two to the man.

Now let us take a look at "The Perfecting of Love" where we again find a dialogue at the beginning of the text—this time in the very opening lines. It goes like this:

"You really can't come?"
"Quite impossible, you know. I must try to get this job finished now as fast as I can."
"But Lilli would be so pleased. . . ."
"I know. Oh I know. But it simply can't be done."
"And I don't like the idea of travelling without you, not a bit . . ."
his wife said as she poured out tea. (Tonka, p. 13; *PSt*, p. 156)[4]

You may ask: What is the point of quoting those two extracts together which, besides the fact that they both are—in part or as a whole—transcriptions of verbal exchanges, have so little in common:

the passionate love-scene on the one side and the trivial, everyday dialogue on the other? However, both passages consist of five utterances, with the same distribution among two interlocuters of different sexes. And there is more. But before we continue, let us read another dialogue of Robert Musil. In the novel *Törless* (and this will be the only time that we cite this celebrated first work of his) there is the following scene: Törless and his classmate Beineberg approach the old bathhouse, now a dubious tavern which houses the prostitute Božena. Frightened by the noise they hear, they both pause, and after a while make out the voices of Božena and one of her visitors:

"You are not going to give me anything, you . . .!"
"Go back into the house, you slut!"
"What? you miserable peasant!"
In response the drunken man lifted a stone with a heavy sweep: "If you don't beat it straightaway, you dumb whore, I'll bash your face in!" and he drew back to throw. Törless heard the woman flee up the stairs with a final curse." (*YT*, p. 33; *PSt*, p. 27)[5]

Although Musil avoids transcribing Božena's last reply, we should note once again that the total number of utterances is five. In other words, that the partner A speaks three times, that partner B twice, as we already found in the former two examples. And now to the other elements common to all three passages. First of all the number of participants and their respective roles. There are three participants: one who watches the action, and two, a man and a woman, who act. Or rather, since the action consists, or mainly consists in a dialogue, a more or less vehement exchange of words, one is the listener, and the other two are speakers. One might question: who is the listener in "The Perfecting of Love," where we have only direct speech, a transcription of the dialogue? The answer, I would say, would be that *we* are the listeners, you and I. Given the form of this dialogue and the way it is introduced, right at the beginning of the tale, we are in a very similar situation as is Törless in the scene just cited or as is the lieutenant listening through the wall. In fact the reader, at the beginning of "The Perfecting of Love" *is* the lieutenant, in the most literal sense of the word, *lieu-tenant*, the one who "holds" the "place," that is, occupies the position of the indiscreet listener, the willing-unwilling intruder in a couple's intimacy. Like the young officer or Törless, the reader too has reason to be puzzled by what he *reads*, just as they were by what they *heard*: he has no idea, at the outset, where these sentences are pronounced, nor to whom the voices belong to—at least until he comes to the point where he reads: "It was his wife who said this as she poured out tea."

Yet if I assert that in all these dialogue-scenes there are three participants, one may still make another objection. In the scene with Božena we have not one but two witnesses: Törless and his companion, Beineberg. However, the strange thing is that Musil, in the central part of this episode seems to forget that, according to the situation he depicts, there *should be* two listeners and only speaks of one: "Törless heard the woman flee up the stairs with a final curse."

Let us take a closer look at the speakers. For it would be wrong to say that they are only distinguished by the fact that they are one male and the other female. Moreover, their mutual relation appears to be one of radical inequality. As you remember, in all three dialogues one partner is in the situation of begging the other to do something (avow his reciprocal love, share the discomfort of a journey or pay his due) which the latter perseveres in refusing. And you will notice that if the one who solicits in *Young Törless* and "The Perfecting of Love" is the woman, in "The Enchanted House" the situation is reversed, the one who denies is the man.

If we now consider the general character of the scene that confronts the bewildered listener, we could characterize it as one of cruelty. Most obviously so in *Young Törless* where the dialogue is on the verge of giving way to physical violence. And in "The Enchanted House," where Victoria's thrice repeated "no!" is explicitly compared to a whip lash. Only in "The Perfecting of Love" does the violence of the refusal seem to be a more secret one.

What could have influenced Musil, in composing these three dialogue-scenes, to follow the same model? As the passage in *Young Törless suggests*, where it entails a slight incoherence in the text, he was probably unaware of the fact, just as the reader of Musil's tales is normally unaware of it.

The aim of psychoanalytical investigation, however, concerns just this point: it seeks to give an account for those achievements of our intellect of which we are unaware. This means that the phenomenon we pointed out might be susceptible to psychoanalytical study. The insistent return of the same pattern in the author's discourse could be interpreted as a "return of the repressed," provided that we are able to show why, in the beginning, the scene in question should have been subject to re-repression.

In the article entitled "On Sexual Theories of Children," Freud shows that children who became witnesses of sexual intercourse between their parents, whatever the detail may be that comes under their observation, "arrive in every case at the same conclusion. They adopt what may be called a *sadistic view of coition*. They see it as something that the stronger participant is forcibly inflicting on the weaker (*etwas das der stärkere Teil dem schwächeren mit Gewalt antut*) and they . . . compare it to the romping familiar to them from their childish experience" (*SE*, 9, p. 221).[6]

This may remind us of our dialogue-scene which, as we just saw, also involves two partners—a man and a woman—of which the weaker (we spoke of him as the soliciting party) regularly submits to the stronger, who denies. And the fact that one of those scenes described by Musil nearly degenerates into a fight and that the other (where it is the woman who has the upper—say—the whip hand) verbal exchange is incidentally compared to a flagellation, also fits rather well into that "sadistic view" of parental love mentioned by Freud.

We should add that the fantasy of watching sexual intercourse between the parents—now usually called the "primal scene"—Freud himself in most cases alludes to as "*Belauschung*," as overhearing the parent's copulation. This could be considered a further indication of the possibility of interpreting the pattern which repeatedly appeared in Musil's narrative discourse as being what Freud calls the typical fantasy seldom absent "among the store of unconscious fantasies of all neurotics, and probably of all human beings" (*SE*, 14, p. 269).

I have some reason to think that the preceding demonstration may not have been altogether convincing, or perhaps that the argumentation is not sufficiently solid. Suppose Musil's first book *Young Törless* is one you have read and still remember; if I assert that in the above mentioned scene with Božena—which you find in the middle of the first third of the book—Törless stands for the author, the prostitute for his mother, the drunkard for his father and their dialogue for sexual intercourse, will you feel that this information—even in case you doubt not of its trustworthiness—in some way or other improves your understanding of that story or of Musil's text as a work of fiction? I am almost certain the answer will be no, and hasten to add—although I believe that if you read the novel again, you might find the interpretation less implausible—that in principle I can only agree with you.

Now let us refer the psychoanalytical interpretation of the dialogue-scene not to a single work, but to the whole sequence of Musil's early fiction-writing. Let us consider both the chronological order of those texts and the point where in each case the scene is located within the story. We will find that in *Törless*, as I just said, it appears in the first third of the story, in "The Enchanted House" on the first page, and in "The Perfecting of Love" in the first line.

Doesn't it seem that with this change of perspective, the interpretation somehow has become more likely?

If you still hesitate, I will ask you to consider the following. If the place of the dialogue moved first from page twenty-seven to page one and then from line fifteen to line one, supposing that the sequence were to be continued (and you know, Musil in fact completed the series by the novella entitled "The Temptation of Quiet Veronica") what do you think could possibly happen next?

Its obvious that the dialogue cannot get any closer to the beginning of the text than it already is in "The Perfecting of Love." If you pushed it further, it would so to say fall out, i.e., just disappear from the story. Continuing our supposition: if the following installment of the dialogue-scene is to overtrump the preceding one, then it must be an intensification of some other kind. At the same time we must also ask what else has changed in the story while the dialogue has been moving closer to the beginning.

One change seems that the dialogue has become more conspicuous. Whereas in *Young Törless* there is nothing which draws particular attention to it, in "The Enchanted House" and all the more in "The Perfecting of Love" the dialogue can hardly be overlooked because of its exposed position. If we now imagine a further version in which the importance of the dialogue-scene in regard to the rest of the story is increased once again, the question is: how could such an increase be brought about? One answer might be: you drop what I just referred to as "all the rest of the story" and only keep the dialogue. More precisely, you compose a novella in the form of a dialogue. Or, in scholarly terms, a novella whose very structure is that of stichomythia, or alternating speech of two interlocutors. That is what Musil, in August, 1910 endeavored to do when he wrote the already mentioned intermediate version of "The Temptation of Quiet Veronica." In this text—let us call it "Veronica I" while referring to the definitive version as "Veronica II"—the heroine and her admirer (now named Johannes) keep a diary together, that is they write by turns in the same notebook. The novella is thus no longer an ordinary narrative, but a juxtaposition of several (here two) narrations in the first person (as one can find in the eighteenth-century epistolary novel for instance).

While he was writing this diary-version of the novella, Musil himself kept a diary. We learn from it that he first made quick progress but then was beset by uncertainty. He found himself faced with questions such as: "What is the point of view of these notes?" "When were they written?" "Why do these people really keep a diary?" and "Do they read each other or not?" The circumstances of this sudden self-criticism, which finally moved the author to dismiss the diary-version of "The Temptation of Quiet Veronica," are peculiar enough to be reported. On the nineteenth of August, 1910, Musil noted: "Strong depressive state for these last three days. I am tired and sometimes dizzy. Above all little confidence in my work. I shall put aside Veronica . . ." (*T*, pp. 220–21).[7] The manuscript of "Veronica I," after the equivalent of thirty typewritten pages stops in the middle of a sentence, somewhere within the sixth diary-entry (with reference to the dialogue-structure we could also say, in the course of the third utterance of partner B). One can propose the following reconstruction: at the moment Musil exceeded the number of five entries, the unconscious factors motivating the use of the diary-form ceased to be effective. Since he forced himself to continue writing, depression accompanied by characteristic physical symptoms set in. The author then desperately sought other justifications for the use of the dialogue-form, failed to find any, but in the process discovered what by realistic standards could only be the total incoherence of the existing manuscript. He therefore rejected it and finally began another version, which was to be the definitive one, and in which he again resorted to narration in the third person.

If you consider once again the various versions of the dialogue, including "Veronica I," you will notice how it becomes increasingly prominent at the expense of what we may call the story, until it finally absorbs the latter entirely. The process reminds one of the invasion of a living organism by disease or by a parasite. A similarity which is for sure not completely fortuituous. For we have good reasons to think that the neuroses which first brought Musil to consult a psychiatrist in Vienna in 1913, as well as the fact that his second book (the novellas), unlike his first, turned out to be a complete flop, were not unrelated to the welling up of his unconscious and the gradual emergence of what we have identified as the "primal fantasy" or "scene."

And yet perhaps this is just the point where our previous discussion lacks in stringency. Although there is more evidence to be discussed in this context, let me first pause to reflect for a moment on the implications of what I have examined so far for the relation between literature and psychoanalysis.

Even if one grants that Musil's early novellas might constitute a suitable object of psychoanalytical investigation, it could be argued that what psychoanalysis in this case applies to are the defective aspects of a work of art. Or put more generally, that Freudian theories could only contribute to what might be called literary pathography. The relation existing between literature and psychoanalysis would then limit itself to borderline or marginal cases to be explained by psychoanalytical theory in a one-sided and irreversible movement.

We will come back to this question later. Let me now return to the question of the primal scene as a possible implication of the recurrent dialogue-scenes in Musil's early narratives. (This will leave open the question whether the use of such a psychoanalytical term must necessarily entail the one-sided movement just referred to.)

The term "primal scene" (*Urszene*) now used to designate the fantasy of watching or listening to the parental intercourse was used by Freud himself only once in the singular form: in his book entitled *From the History of an Infantile Neurosis*. The term is apparently introduced there in order to emphasize that the "scene" in question was precisely not a fantasy.

The most crucial element of this psychoanalysis, referred to as the "Wolfman," is a nightmare the patient first had at the age of four and which was repeated during the period of his treatment with Freud. In the dream the Wolfman is lying in bed as the window opens, sees a number of white wolves sitting on a big tree; terrified of being devoured, he screams and wakes up.

Behind this dream—the interpretation of which took several

years—Freud discovered the primal scene: at the age of one and a half years, while still sharing his parents' bedroom, the patient woke up one afternoon at five and witnessed a coitus repeated three times. We see that the numbers that occupy such a prominent part in Musil's dialogue-scenes (*five* utterances, *three* participants) can also be found in the primal scene Freud constructs in the Wolfman case (*five* o'clock, *three* times repeated coitus).

The parallel is striking. Is it only a coincidence? According to Freud, the numbers *five* and *three* proceed from real events in the patient's life. From the age of ten and continuing into the psychoanalysis, the Wolfman was affected by "modes of depression," which "used to come in the afternoon and reached their height at about five o'clock" (*SE*, 17, p. 37). This symptom, Freud suggests, actually derives from the traumatic experience his patient had in early childhood. The depression culminates at five o'clock *because* that was the hour at which he witnessed his parents' copulation. In other words, the numbers *five* and *three* indicate the points where the primal scene inserts itself into reality and so help to authenticate the Wolfman's experience.

If these numbers indicate the reality of the scene here and if our interpretation of Musil's dialogues is accepted, might not a similar possibility be applicable there as well? Might not Musil also have happened to watch his parents perform coitus three times one day around the hour of five (or perhaps inversely at the hour of three and then five times)? An extravagent supposition, no doubt. But perhaps it may be a little bit less extravagant to suggest that the numbers *five* and *three*, as found for instance in Musil's text, comprise an integral part of what Freud usually calls "primal fantasy." In other words, that they appear in the Wolfman's psychoanalysis not for realistic, empirical reasons, but for structural ones.

Yet, if the link existing between the primal scene and the numbers *five* and *three* is not based on the fortuitous facts of individual experience, its nature still needs to be elucidated. In fact, this sort of problem is precisely what Freud himself was preoccupied with when he wrote the case-study. From the beginning he declares that the Wolfman was one of those rare cases where analysis succeeds "in descending into the deepest and most primitive strata of mental development" (*SE*, 17, p. 10), and at the end of the book he raises the question of what he will then refer to as being the "nucleus of the unconscious" (*SE*, 17, p. 120). "If one considers," he writes, "the behaviour of the four-year-old child towards the re-activated primal scene, or even, if one thinks of the far simpler reactions of the one-and-a-half-year-old child when the scene was actually experienced, it is hard to dismiss the view that some sort of hardly definable knowledge, something, as it were, preparatory to an understanding was at work in the child at that time" (ibid.). You will have noted, although Freud still maintains that the primal scene, in the Wolfman case, was a matter of experience, he nevertheless grants that it had to be preceded by something else, prior to all experience. As to the question of what this knowledge previous to all knowledge might be, Freud acknowledges a dilemma. "We can form no conception," he says, "of what this may have consisted in" (ibid.), but in the same breath proposes what he calls an "excellent" analogy: "the far-reaching *instinctive* knowledge of animals" (ibid.). A few lines earlier, he had already put forward another explanation, referring to "the phylogenetically inherited schemata which, like the categories of philosophy," are concerned with the business of 'placing' the impressions derived from actual experience" (*SE*, 17, p. 119). As an example of such a schema, Freud then mentioned "the Oedipus complex, which comprises a child's relation to his parents" and showed that, precisely in the case of the Wolfman, we are "able to see the schema triumphing over the experience of the individual" (ibid.).

Freud's two attempts to account for the preprogrammation of individual experience as situated in the "nucleus of the unconscious" have, half a century later, in the course of what shall be named a "return to Freud," been called into question by the French psychoanalyst Jacques Lacan, who offers a quite different explanation. "It is only a makeshift device (*un artifice*)," he writes for instance concerning the Oedipus complex, "to invoke in this respect the product of hereditary amnesia (*un acquis amnésique héréditaire*)" (*Ecrits*, p. 686)[8] and again, "The unconscious is neither the primordial nor the instinctual and is only elementary insofar as it entails elements of the signifier" (*Ecrits*, p. 522). The key to that knowledge prior to all knowledge of which Freud speaks is provided by the structure of the signifier which, for Lacan, determines the signified, or as we may say here, the knowledge.

Let us, once again, return to our former argument. You shall have noted that the application of Freudian theory to a work of literature may, in some cases, rebound upon the theory itself. The material supplied by Musil's early novellas is one which calls into question the efforts Freud makes in the Wolfman case to convince both himself and his readers of the (exceptional) traumatic origin of the primal scene. The relation between literature and psychoanalysis therefore can no longer be regarded here as a unilateral one. It is not just psychoanalysis which informs literature, but also literature which transforms psychoanalysis. We should not neglect to emphasize how this change of perspective was brought about. The reason, simply, is that we no longer referred to Freudian theory *in general*, but to one of Freud's writings in particular. We began to juxtapose two texts besides their obvious difference in nature. And that is what I shall continue to do.

When I remarked earlier that Musil at one moment broke off work on the manuscript of the diary-version of "Veronica I" and later replaced it by a definitive one, I omitted to mention that "Veronica I" contained one element apparently so dear to its author that he could not bring himself to discard it, but, instead, retained it in "Veronica II," despite the fact that it was out of place there and of no functional use whatsoever, except to add to the perplexity generally provoked by this novella in its readers. This element, which migrated, with only a few trifling alterations, from the penultimate into the ultimate version of "The Temptation of Quiet Veronica," is the opening paragraph, a sort of prelude or preamble to the story itself. This passage served formerly as something like an editorial introduction presenting Veronica's and Johannes' intimate diary to the public. It goes like this:

Somewhere there are two voices. Perhaps they merely lie mute on the pages of a diary, now side by side, now intertwining, according as the pages come: the woman's a dark deep voice that is from the first instant rounded, self-collected, and yet enclosed by the mellow, expansive, ever expanding voice of the man, and the man's voice with many ramifications, like a thing unfinished, the sound of it revealing all that the speaker has had no time to conceal. Or perhaps not even that. Or perhaps after all there is, somewhere in the world, a point towards which these two voices—scarcely distinguishable as they are amid the dull confusion of everyday humdrum noises—dart like two rays of light, there at last to mingle. Perhaps one should feel the need to search for that point, which may be nearer than one thinks, though it betrays its nearness only in a stirring like that of a music not yet audible, but already imprinted, in heavy folds vaguely outlined in the still impenetrable curtain of things far off. If one found it, perhaps these scattered fragments here would once more assume their wholeness, would shed their malady and weakness, and stand erect and firm in the lucidity of day. (*Tonka*, p. 68)

And here's how it sounds in German:

Irgendwo muß man zwei Stimmen hören. Vielleicht liegen sie bloß wie stumm auf den Blättern eines Tagebuchs nebeneinander und ineinander, die dunkle, tiefe, plötzlich mit einem Sprung um sich selbst gestellte Stimme der Frau, wie die Seiten es fügen, von der weichen, weiten, gedehnten Stimme des Mannes umschlossen, von dieser verästelt, unferug gebliebenen liegen Stimme, zwischen der das, was sie noch nicht zu bedecken Zeit fand, hervorschaut. Vielleicht auch dies nicht. Vielleicht aber gibt es irgendwo in der Welt einen Punkt, wohin diese zwei, überall sonst aus der matten Verwirrung der alltäglichen Geräusche sich kaum hebenden heraus Stimmen wie zwei Strahlen schießen und sich ineinanderschlingen, irgendwo, vielleicht sollte man diesen Punkt suchen wollen, dessen Nähe man hier nur an einer Unruhe gewahrt wie die Bewegung einer Musik, die noch nicht hörbar, sich schon mit schweren unklaren Falten in dem undurchrissenen Vorhang der Ferne abdrückt. Vielleicht daß diese Stücke hier dann aneinandersprängen, aus ihrer Krankheit und Schwäche hinweg ins Klare, Tagfeste, Aufgerichtete. (*PSt*, p. 194)[9]

You will certainly have noticed the insistent repetition of the words *vielleicht* ("perhaps") and *irgendwo* ("somewhere"). The former recurs *five* times, the latter *three* times, and that shall probably not surprise you anymore. Even if I add that the entire paragraph is divided into *five* parts, the number of sentences it includes. At the risk of trying your patience beyond endurance, I will call your attention to the fact that the title, which immediately proceeds this passage consists of *five* words: Die Versuchung der stillen Veronika. And, although I regret having to continue along this line, that the manuscript of "Veronica I," on top of the page, still showed the overall title of the book, which happens to be a word of *five* syllables, "Ver-ei-ni-gun-gen." Finally I am quite embarrassed to point out that this fivefold articulation successively applies to three levels of language: sentence, word, syllable.

But let us change the subject. You may also have noted that the text shows a certain predilection for alliteration or, as it is called in German, *Stabreim*. As you probably know, in German alliteration is characterized by the fact that all initial sounds (both of words and lexemes) have a stronger accent. If we go any further into this matter here, we would come to the conclusion that with the exception of alliteration in /d/ (the high frequency of which is due to its presence in such—inevitable—words as the different forms of the article, "*der, die, das*" and the pronouns derived from it) the most frequent forms of alliteration involve the phonemes /f/ (*Vorhang der Ferne*) and /v/ (*irgendwo in der Welt*) or combinations of those two initial sounds (*von der weichen, weiten . . .; Verwirrung*). More precisely, it appears that in this text three sounds, the fricatives /f/ and /v/ and the sibilant /ʃ/, are, by far, the most frequent ones in the initial. Each can be counted exactly seventeen times, whereas no other phoneme (/d/ excepted) occurs more than twelve times in that position. We thus find that in this regard as well, the preamble and the title of the novella agree perfectly with each other, since there is the same distribution of these initial sounds to be found here and there: D*ie* V*ersuchung der* S*tillen* V*eronika*.

While we are examining the title of the story we might mention another fact, concerning both its phonological and its typographical components. The letter V, which appears in the initial of V*ersuchung* and in that of V*eronika* is in the latter case voiced and in the former voiceless. This demonstrates the phonological ambiguity of this sign in the German alphabet. We should also note that in the heading *Die Versuchung der stillen Veronika* the grapheme V manifestly occupies a dominant position both as the only capital letter and because of its double occurence at the beginning and at the end of the line. Nor should it be forgotten that a capital V (to complete another triad!) again appears in the title of the book.

The word *Vereinigungen* however deserves even closer examination in another regard. Apparently, there is a direct relation between this programmatic term and the process described in the programmatic opening passage of "The Temptation of Quiet Veronica:" the two voices, male and female, are compared to two "rays of light," "darting" towards a "point" where they "mingle." You will agree that if you tried to draw such a thing you could only trace a more or less acute angle, i.e., a figure corresponding to the letter V.

The V then not only stands for the principal sounds of that passage, but at the same time can be regarded as being an emblem or pictogram of the central notion of "union" or, as we should better say in English, "conjunction."

But what about the numbers *three* and *five*? Doesn't the V form a figure connecting three points? As for *five*, just consider the V as Roman numeral.

Thus the V, phonetic symbol, numeral and emblem all at the same time, appears as the common denominator of all those salient features included in the preamble of Musil's novella, "The Temptation of Quiet Veronica," connecting that passage both with the work and the book-title. And what if the link which exists between the numbers *three* and *five* occurring in the primal scene (in Musil's and the Wolfman's) wasn't any other than the letter V, that is to say, one of those elements of the signifier Lacan speaks about. For that is indeed what, according to him, one *should* expect to find in the "nucleus of the unconscious."

But perhaps you are not quite ready yet to grant that the various connections existing between Musil's novella and the letter V should be an achievement of the author's unconscious. After all, he might have introduced them deliberately. And since in a letter he wrote in April, 1942, a few days before he died, he in fact speaks of an "almost artistic esoteric doctrine" (*eine fast künstlerische Geheimlehre*) (PSt, p. 832) to be found in that book, does not such a conscious intention seem even more likely? A comparison of the two existing versions of the preamble will prove on the contrary, that it is highly improbable that Musil knew what he was doing when he introduced those features, notably the numerical pattern, into his text.

I have, thus far, not mentioned another pecularity of this passage: the fact that the word *"Punkt"* (point) in the sentence "perhaps . . . there is, somewhere in the world, a point . . ." occurs precisely in the middle of this text consisting of 161 words, of which *"Punkt"* is the eighty-first, which means that it is both preceded and followed by exactly 80 words. And that, I hope you will agree, is unlikely to be the result of mere accident. Now, the point is . . . that in the older version, the term "Punkt" appeared in the seventy-third position whereas the total number of words, there too, was already 161. Moreover, in "Veronica I," we only have 4 sentences instead of 5 and 16 initial /ʃ/ phonemes instead of 17. So the balance and symmetry of those numerical relations only became perfect in the course of the last revision of the text. Assuming that they were established deliberately, we must consider that the author, when composing this passage, actually *counted* the sentences, words and initial phonemes it contains. And if that were the case, why shouldn't he have established those numerical relations from the outset? Why should he first have made such crass mistakes in counting? It seems increasingly difficult not holding the unconscious responsible for all these number games. In any case, this is what the close correspondence with the Wolfman's medical history tends to suggest.

When I earlier spoke of the letter V as an emblem or pictograph, those familiar with Freud's book, will already have been reminded of the passage in which we learn how the Wolfman's phobia of butterflies became comprehensible the day he remarked that what was actually frightening him was the opening and shutting of the butterfly's wings. The recalled "a woman opening her legs," which "made the shape of a Roman V," the hour, Freud adds, "at which . . . the Wolfman used to fall into a depressed state of mind" (*SE*, 17, p. 90).

Just as in the case of Musil, the letter V here appears to be the center of a whole network of relations and simultaneously to function both as the figure of a pair of wings or legs and as a numeral (the Roman numeral V). On other occasions, for instance when the patient dreams of *Wölfe* ("wolves") or of a *Wespe* ("wasp") the V is present in the initial W of the two words as representant of the initial fricative /v/. Finally, concerning the V as numeral, far from occuring only once, in connection with the primal scene, the numbers *three* and *five* persistently return in the patient's statements and several times, accompanied by such strange circumstances, that one wonders how this predilection could have escaped Freud's attention and thus remain uninterpreted. (Most remarkable is, in connection with the primal scene, the fact that the patient at one moment maintained that the *three-fold* repetition of the parental coitus was a detail which had been suggested to him by Freud [which the latter explicitly denied]. Apparently, the number *three* he had mentioned in this context, subsequently sounded so alien to him, that he could not avoid attributing it to the Other—here represented by the psychoanalyst).

Summing up, what Freud's (and his patient's) psychoanalytical investigation brings to light, is the same unconscious pattern which Musil's early novellas gradually focused on: a network of interconnected elements centered on the letter V of which the fantasy of the primal scene is only one manifestation.

The fact that in both cases the pattern is the same does not by any means mean that the form in which it appears in Musil and in Freud will also be identical. What is striking is rather the difference that emerges between the text of Freud and that of Musil. In Musil's text the pattern is inscribed with such clarity and emphasis that its appearence in Freud seems vague by comparison and in fact its overall significance can only be discerned when Freud's text is juxtaposed with that of Musil. This difference recalls Freud's remark in his essay on Jensen's "Gradiva" that "creative writers (*Dichter*) are far in advance of us everyday people in their knowledge of the mind" (*SE*, 9, p. 8) and further, with reference to Shakespeare's *Hamlet* that their evidence is "to be prized highly, for they are apt to know a whole host of things between heaven and earth of which our philosophy has not yet let us dream" (ibid.).

What kind of knowing then do we actually find in Musil's text? Nothing other than that "hardly definable knowledge," something "preparatory to an understanding" mentioned by Freud in the last chapter of the "Wolfman." And if one asks what is the object of this knowing, one can only answer that it consists in the constellation of three phonemes (/f/, /v/, and /ʃ/) which plays such a prominent role in the pattern we have decerned. A phonemic *pair* on the one hand, whose components are distinguished from one another merely by the voiced-unvoiced *opposition*. On the other hand, the third component, a *single* sound, which in the phonemic system of Austria and south Germany is characterized by the fact that the opposition between voiced and unvoiced is neutralized. That is, this sound operates as *un undicidable* marker. Such indecidability articulates the uncertainty of one's own sex together with the Oedipus complex.

This suggests that the letter V might represent the difference of the sexes as such. In other words, it serves as representative of the phallus. The reason that such knowledge could articulate itself so graphically may well be that Musil, unlike Freud, was not constrained to communicate it directly in a conceptual comprehensible form. And, the consequence of this indirect form of articulation can be seen in the following notes of Musil. In 1918, he writes concerning his novellas: "They don't develop—they envelope (*sie entfalten nicht, sie falten ein*). Their essence and why they were not understood. A poetic fiction (*Dichtung*), not narration" (*T*, p. 350). Development here ascribed to narration is opposed to envelopment atributed to *"Dichtung."* Apparently, this characterization is meant to account for the non-narrative aspect of *Vereinigungen*, a quality which these texts acquired at the expense of the story. But then, what does the notion of "enveloping" finally drive at? Another note of Musil from an autobiographical fragment written around 1936 might give us a hint. He designates his second book as a "carefully executed text (*eine sorgfältig ausgeführte Schrift*) which, when viewed through a magnifying glass . . . would contain many times its apparent content" (*T*, p. 809). This "compactness" then seems to be what the "enveloping" in the case of *Vereinigungen* leads to. If we look for something that exemplifies the concentration Musil is here describing, we could hardly do better than the dream, which Freud designates as a result of condensation. That is to say, Musil's definition of his book, *Vereinigungen*, as "*Dichtung*" in fact indicates its "density" proceeding from the operation of "condensation," of "*Ver-Dichtung*" in the Freudian sense of the term. Condensation, here we should specify, is taken to the ultimate degree, that of one individual *letter*.

All of which might be summed up by saying that the marginality of Musil's text, which makes it accessible to a psychoanalytical reading, could well be the marginality of *literature* itself.

NOTES

1. Robert Musil, *Prosa und Stücke, kleine Prosa, Aphorismen, Autobiographisches, Essays und Reden*, ed. Adolf Frisé (Hamburg: Rowohlt, 1978). Quotations of Musil's fiction are from this collection and will be indicated parenthetically in the text by the abbreviation *PSt*. Translations of the quotes are by Peter Henninger unless otherwise noted.

2. Burton E. Pike, *Robert Musil: An Introduction to His Work* (Ithaca, N.Y.: Cornell University Press, 1961), p. 67.

3. Ibid., p. 69.

4. Robert Musil, *Tonka and Other Stories*, trans. Eithne Wilkins and Ernst Kaiser (London: Secker and Warburg, 1955). References are to both the English and German to indicate that the translation has been modified.

5. Robert Musil, *Young Törless*, trans. Eithne Wilkins and Ernst Kaiser (New York: Pantheon Books, 1955).

6. Sigmund Freud, *The Standard Edition of the Complete Psychological Works of Sigmund Freud*, trans. James Strachey, 24 vols. (London: Hogarth Press, 1953–74). Quotations of Freud will be indicated parenthetically in the text by the abbreviation *SE*.

7. Robert Musil, *Tagebücher*, ed. Adolf Frisé (Hamburg: Rowohlt, 1976). Quotations from this collection will be noted parenthetically as *T*; translations are by Peter Henninger.

8. Jacques Lacan, *Écrits* (Paris: Seuil, 1966). Quotations of Lacan will be indicated parenthetically in the text by the title: translations are by Peter Henninger.

9. In this transcription Musil's own spelling has been reestablished on the authority of his manuscript No. iv, 2, 369 (catalogue Kaiser/Wilkins; Albertson/Corino).

NOTES ON CONTRIBUTORS

MITCHELL BREITWIESER is a graduate student in the English department at the State University of New York at Buffalo. He is currently completing a dissertation on American historiography and hermeneutics entitled "Plastic Economy: The Projects of Cotton Mather and Walt Whitman."

PETER HENNINGER teaches German at the University of Paris-X (Nanterre). He is the author of "Der Buchstabe und der Geist" (on Robert Musil; forthcoming from Stuttgart) and is currently preparing "Ecriture et Inconscient," a study of Nietzsche, Freud, and Musil.

LAURENCE B. HOLLAND is a professor of American literature and the chairman of the English department at The Johns Hopkins University. He is the author of *The Expense of Vision: Essays on the Craft of Henry James* and the editor of the new *Norton Anthology of American Literature*.

WILLIAM LEVITAN is a graduate student in classics at the University of Texas at Austin. "Plexed Artistry" is part of a longer study of ancient poetry entitled "The Field of Roman Verse."

RAINER NÄGELE is an associate professor of German at The Johns Hopkins University. His publications include *Literatur und Utopie*.

Versuche zu Hölderlin and several books and articles on eighteenth-century and modern German literature. He is presently working on a new book dealing with Hölderlin and problems of poetic signification, tentatively titled "Text and History."

EDUARDO SACCONE is a professor of Italian at The Johns Hopkins University. The author of *Commento a "Zeno," Il soggetto del "Furioso,"* and *Il poeta travestito*, he is currently working on "Good and Bad Manners," essays on Castiglione and Della Casa, and "Unwise Couplings," a triptych on novelists Palazzeschi, Tozzi, and Gadda.